PIPPA GOODHART

THE GREAT

SEA DRAGON DISCOVERY

Catnip
PUBLISHING LTD

CATNIP BOOKS
Published by Catnip Publishing Ltd
320 City Road
London
EC1V 2NZ

This edition first published 2018

1 3 5 7 9 10 8 6 4 2

A CIP catalogue record for this book is available from the British Library.

ISBN 978-1-910611-08-1

Printed and bound by CPI Group (UK) Ltd., Croydon, CR0 4YY

www.catnippublishing.co.uk

For the Sedgwick Museum in Cambridge,
which makes so many fossils and stories
available to us all.

Chapter One

Grantchester, September 1860

The daisy on Miss Snelling's desk was wilting in the heat. Bruisewort. It was old Mrs Coddle in the village who called daisies bruisewort. She said their juice would cure bruises or keep a cut clean. But Dad had told Bill that 'daisy' was really 'day's eye', because the flower opened in daylight but closed at night. Bill had picked this one in the school lunch break, from a patch of grass where he and the others sat to eat and chat. Coming back into the schoolroom for afternoon lessons, he'd popped the daisy into the ink well on Miss Snelling's desk. He could see it now, flopped over but still with petals spread wide. Would a plant drink ink as happily as it would drink water? Or would the ink kill it? By the end of the afternoon he'd know.

Bill was as thirsty as the daisy. It was too hot in that small classroom with a hundred children crammed in. There was a new lot who had only arrived in the school that day. The Smiths. Eight of them, so that now everyone was squashed tighter than ever onto the school benches. The sour smell of hot, grubby bodies made Bill long to be outside again. At least his end of the bench was near the window. Bill squinted into the sunlight shining through the diamond panes, watching a farm cart being pulled down the road by a big white horse.

He recognized the horse. Dolly. For the last couple of weeks, Bill had been out helping with the harvest, raking the cut wheat, tying it in stooks, then pitching it up onto the cart being pulled by big Dolly. Bill would have been happy to carry on with the farm work, but Ma said he had to get his education and go back to school.

'I've brought you up for something better than farm work,' she said. 'I want to see you in a nice, warm, indoor job with a steady income, Billy. A bank, maybe.'

But Bill wasn't interested in what was taught in school. The teacher, Miss Snelling, droned on like a trapped bluebottle. Dressed in her shiny dark-blue bodice and long skirt, she even looked like the dead bluebottle tangled in the spider's web on the corner of the window beside him. With ringlets damply dangling either side of her sharp face, Miss Snelling stood stiffly beside the blackboard.

Curly letters emerged, tapping and shrieking, from her white chalk as she talked.

'Who can tell me . . . ?' she said.

. . . why it is that flies eat rotting stuff, and then a spider eats the flies, and a bird eats the spider, and a cat eats the bird, and . . . does anything eat a cat? wondered Bill. *A big fox might eat a small cat, but then did anything eat a fox? Or did it all just go back to maggots, if the fox died without being eaten by anything? Maggots would turn into flies again, of course . . .*

Bill was watching a plump spider working at its web. *It's saving the fly to eat later,* he thought.

Miss Snelling was reading from the Bible now, a passage from Job about somebody's trust which 'shall be a spider's web', apparently meaning that the trust was weak.

But a spider's web isn't weak, thought Bill. He poked the web on the window, and it moved but didn't break. Back and forth went the spider, adding spokes and braces, all evenly spaced. *How did any spider know how to make such a perfect sticky net for catching flies? Did an older spider teach the young ones how to do it? In a spider school? If insects could teach their young things like that, then why don't flies know that they should keep away from spider webs? Are spiders cleverer than flies? Perhaps the flies get caught and die before they can ever warn the y–*

'William Ellwood!'

Bill jerked upright. Miss Snelling was staring at him, eyebrows raised, her chalk pointing at him.

'For the benefit of everyone here, you are please to repeat what I have just said.' Miss Snelling's voice was dangerously quiet, her face glowing damp with the heat. The children silently watched Bill, some of them blowing upwards to get hot hair off their eyes.

Bill's mouth opened. He knew exactly what Miss Snelling had just been saying. It was, 'For the benefit of everyone here, you are please to repeat what I have just said,' but he also knew that she didn't want that truth. She wanted something she'd said before that, and he had no idea what it could be.

'Er . . .'

Bill tried to peer around Miss Snelling and the big girl monitor, to see what was chalked on the blackboard, but the monitor was deliberately shielding it from him. She was smirking. Other children were giggling behind their hands. Bill felt himself blush. What *had* she said?

'Well?' Miss Snelling's eyebrows were up.

'That dreaming is for night time, Miss,' said Bill. That was something she often did say to him.

Miss Snelling's mouth twitched, and the chalk was lowered. 'That was *not* what I said, William, but it is what I was *about* to say, so maybe your powers of telling the future will save you, this time,' said Miss Snelling. She turned once again to the board.

Ping!

'Oi!' shouted Bill, slapping a hand to his neck where something had hit him. He saw straight away who must have done it. It was one of those new children. The boy twisted around and looked at Bill with a sneer that gave him away even though his arms were down at his sides. He stuck his tongue out just a bit, showing Bill another pellet of chewed paper ready to be spat. Bill lunged at him.

'William Ellwood!' Miss Snelling had gone beetroot red in the face. 'You are a disgrace! And after I let the other incident go! I will not have fighting in class, nor such treatment of a new child. Come to the front.' Miss Snelling reached for her cane.

Bill left school that afternoon with his palms stinging hot. Miss Snelling might be a lady, but she could whack a cane fast enough to cut flesh like a knife. He'd kept his mouth shut tight as she hit him, not wanting to give that boy the satisfaction of knowing how much hurt he'd caused. Afterwards, Bill had sat back on the bench and focused his attention on the daisy still in Miss Snelling's inkwell. He watched the blue of the ink seeping into the white petals until what had been white was all blue and the school day was over.

Clamping his stinging palms under opposite armpits, Bill dodged out of school as soon as the monitor rang the bell.

'Show us your hands, then!' said Ted Dilley, grabbing Bill's arm as he tried to set off home. 'I counted! Have you got six stripes? Did they bleed?'

The other village boys were dancing around him too.

'Get off!' Bill hunched out of Ted's grip. He could see that paper-pellet-spitting new boy coming out of the door. He was with some other boys and a couple of small girls with the same distinct curly hair that was somewhere in between black and ginger. The girls, in grubby pinafores, looked as fierce as the boys did. The boy who had got Bill into trouble took a step towards him now, and asked, 'Who are you looking at, Billy Ellwood?'

'Go on, fight him, Bill!' said Ted. But Bill couldn't have fought the whole family army of them even if he'd wanted to, and he didn't. He just wanted to get away from them.

Miss Snelling stepped out of the school room. 'Off you go, children.' She wafted then clapped her hands, as if she was chasing chickens.

Bill ran off, but the sound of running footsteps behind him made him glance over his shoulder. The Smith boy was following. Did the boy want a fight? Bill certainly didn't.

The boy was smaller than Bill; could Bill outrun him?

Avoiding home now, Bill made for the meadows and the river, scrambling over the gate and running through the long grass, leading the boy away from the other children.

'Oi, you! Scaredy!' the boy shouted as he chased after Bill. He sounded fierce – and close. He might be small, but he was clearly fast.

I wonder if he can swim? thought Bill.

Bill ran down the grassy slope to the river, swung out his arms and dived in. He plunged down into the cold water which muffled sights and sounds. Ma hadn't made Bill wear his boots today, since it was hot, so now he flip-flapped his feet and worked his arms to power away from the bank. He felt calm in this cool different world.

Something sploshed beside him – a clod of mud thrown from the riverbank. *So he can't swim,* thought Bill. *Good!* He popped his head above the water, looked back and grinned at the boy, then took a deep breath and dived under the water again, gliding over the wavery green weeds of the riverbed, the sunlight sparkling on the silver skin of the water above him. Kicking upstream, he surfaced, and twisted onto his back to look downstream. Two of the boy's brothers and a sister had joined him on the bank now. They were chasing each other, but that boy had his hand to his brow to shade his eyes, watching Bill. Bill flipped over and swam on, around the corner and away.

Then he lay on his back, floating, and his thoughts floated free too. The water held Bill up, so long as he kept flat. But how did it do that? Bill had watched water boatmen skating over water, denting the surface but never falling down into it. Bill thought of the cream rising to the top of the milk in the jug on Ma's cold slab, making a skin of a thicker sort of milk. But water didn't get thicker at the top, did it? So how could it have a skin?

Bill looked up at the browning, rustling leaves of the big chestnut trees on the riverbank. *Summer's ending,* he thought. A bright, turquoise flash of a kingfisher darted over the greenery of the bank. He turned and swam towards the mill, the rush and rumble of water in its wheels growing louder the nearer he got. He was intending to get out on the shallow bank of the mill pond, but there were two figures walking beside the river, in Mr Widnall's garden. The straw hat and beard belonged to Mr Widnall himself. Bill's dad worked for Mr Widnall as a nurseryman, growing dahlias. The other figure, dusted in white flour, was the miller, Mr Nutter. Bill didn't want to have to explain being in the river in his clothes, so he paused in the reeds and listened to their talk, waiting for them to move away.

Mr Widnall waved his arms as he spoke. 'Coprolites are changing the village,' he said. 'You must have seen the new labourers around the place, here for the diggings.

Men from who knows where?'

Bill thought of the Smith family. Had they come to find work at the coprolite diggings? He'd watched the workers dig the dark stony lumps from the ground and load them into carts to be taken away to where they would be made into fertiliser for fields. He'd enjoyed the arrival of new machines and new people into the village, until today.

'It's putting an end to our flower business, I'm afraid,' said Mr Widnall. 'Those acres of flowers that my father simply doted on . . . well, they are to be no more.'

'Surely the flower fields can be spared?' said Mr Nutter.

'Seemingly not,' said Mr Widnall. 'Surveyors have tested the ground, and exactly those fields are the ones that are rich in the coprolite nodules. Maybe that's why the flowers grow so well there? We don't own the land, of course, and King's College seem to have more loyalty to money than they do to my mother or myself. What do you think of that, eh?'

'Could the flower growing move elsewhere?' asked Mr Nutter.

Mr Widnall made a harrumphing sort of sound. Bill shivered in the shaded, chill water. He wanted to get out, but needed to hear more. If Mr Widnall's flower growing moved, would Dad's job move too?

'Moving the flower growing would be a huge labour,'

said Mr Widnall, 'and for a business which isn't as keen as it once was . . . Maybe, after all, this will prove to be a blessing in disguise. The truth is, I'm busy with other interests, and the flowers have taken more time than I have wanted to give them these last few years. With fewer acres and fewer workmen to worry over, my time will be more my own.'

'So, which of your men will you let go?'

Bill held his breath. That was exactly what he wanted to know too.

'It will have to be the flower specialist chaps. Hard on them, of course, but I expect they'll find work with the coprolite companies. I'll need just one good nurseryman, to supervise what will be left in the greenhouses and so on. Other than that, I can use my farm labourers to help out when necessary.'

One good nurseryman, thought Bill. Dad certainly was 'a good nurseryman', but was he the very best of the men who worked on Mr Widnall's flowers? Dad, with his clumsy club foot, had worked long, patient, mostly happy, hours since he was twelve years old, first for Mr Widnall's father, who was a great grower and breeder of dahlias, and then for the younger Mr Widnall, whose heart was more given over to making and inventing than flower growing. Only Mr Ballard had worked for the Widnalls longer than Dad had, but he was old. The other men were stronger than either Dad or Mr Ballard, but not so experienced. *Which of those things would matter most when Mr Widnall made his choice?* Bill wondered. What would happen if Dad lost the job that earned Bill's family's living? Bill wanted to rise up out of the water and tell Mr Widnall that he *must* keep Dad in his job. But showing himself to be an eavesdropper, as well as dripping wet as he pleaded for Dad's job, would embarrass Dad, and maybe even spoil his chances of staying on. So Bill stayed silent and still in the water, shivering.

It was only when the two men finally moved towards the house that Bill pulled himself out of the water, weighed down by wet clothes and worry. He hurried home, running soggily and avoiding people. *I must warn Dad*, he thought. With Ma unwell, they needed money for the doctor as well as the usual rent and food costs.

Bill jumped over the rabbit-proof fence into his back yard, landing amongst squawking chickens. He ran straight into the lean-to back scullery, through to the main room – where he came to an abrupt halt, dripping onto the brick floor. In front of him was not just Ma, but the vicar's wife, Mrs Buckle, who sniffed and wrinkled her nose with disgust when she saw him.

'Billy!' said Ma. 'Where have you. . . ? Oh, my gracious! Oh, I'm so sorry, Mrs Buckle.'

'I went swimming,' said Bill, wondering why that nosy

woman was in his house anyway. 'I was hot.'

'But why ever didn't you . . . ? Whatever must you think of us, Mrs Buckle?' Ma always particularly minded about Bill being 'proper' in the company of social superiors. Bill thought it was for the guests to do the behaving, if they were in his home.

Mrs Buckle sat up very straight in Pa's Windsor chair, her mouth tightly disapproving and her eyes now firmly averted from the sight of dripping Bill. Ma, who should have been sitting down and resting as the doctor had instructed, was now standing to pour tea into the pink and white best china teacup, which had come from her mother.

'Go and change at once, Billy! Mrs Buckle is kindly here to help with . . . Oh.' Ma's voice faltered, and Bill knew that she had stopped talking so as not to let out a sob.

'Ma?'

'Something's happened. Something upsetting.' Ma looked at Bill with big wet eyes. 'Go and dry yourself and I'll tell you when you come back down.'

So Bill lifted the latch of the door in the corner, and hurried up the steep, dark stairs to his parents' room, and then on up the ladder to his own tiny room in the roof, where he peeled off wet clothes and pulled on dry ones, his head spinning with what might have upset

Ma so much. His being wet in front of the vicar's wife couldn't be all of it. There must be something else . . .

Bill sat down hard on his bed. Had Dad already lost his job?

Chapter Two

Mrs Buckle was leaving as Bill crept back down the stairs. He waited, watching Ma almost bobbing a curtsey, thanking Mrs Buckle for coming, and then closing the door and crumpling down into her chair, hands to her face as a sob at last escaped from her mouth.

'Ma? What is it?'

Bill put an arm around his mother's thin shoulders. They were draped in the faded paisley shawl she'd been handed down by the last lady she worked for. She must have snatched it to cover over her tired brown work dress, when she saw Mrs Buckle at the door. Ma leaned her head against him.

'Don't ask me, Billy, because I can't tell you anything until your father is home,' she said.

So it is to do with Dad, thought Bill. He took a deep

breath. 'I'll make dinner, shall I, Ma? I can cook some spuds and –'

'Oh, my Billy. Don't leave me,' said Ma, suddenly clutching him tight.

'The spuds are only in the bucket out the back!' said Bill.

'That's not . . . Oh, take no notice of me!' said Ma, sitting up straighter. 'Yes, love, you get those potatoes cooking or your father will think –'

'What will his father think?' William Ellwood stepped through the doorway, sweeping his cap off his thinning fair hair and tossing it expertly onto its peg on the wall.

He's not lost his job if he's that cheerful! thought Bill.

Dad grinned. 'Mr Widnall's asked me to choose his exhibit for best single dahlia bloom in next Saturday's show,' he said. 'What do you think of that, eh? I've got in mind to display . . .' Then Dad stopped talking, noticing Ma's white face. 'Why, what's the matter Sally girl?' Dad reached out a hand to her. Ma just shook her head, unable to speak.

'Mrs Buckle was here, saying something,' said Bill. 'It's upset Ma.' Perhaps Ma knew more about Dad's job than Dad did.

'It's Lily,' sobbed Ma, gazing into Dad's face.

'Lily?' said Bill, surprised. 'Who's Lily?'

'My sister,' said Ma, turning to him. 'My little sister,

who I've not seen for years. She's your . . . Well, she's your Aunt Lily, Billy. Your aunt. Lil and your Uncle Fred have come back to the village. Mrs Buckle came to tell me, because Lil had told her that we are related. Oh, I was so embarrassed! Lil and Fred and all those children are so . . . well, so common.'

'Oh, Ma!'

'Well then,' said Dad, sitting down. 'It's not so bad, is it? But why have they come back here just now, do you know?'

'Fred's landed a job working the coprolites, Mrs Buckle says. They've all moved into old Mrs Dorley's place on Bugs Row. Arrived yesterday. Thirteen of them now, would you believe!'

With a cold trickle of dread down his insides, Bill asked, 'Are Aunt Lily's family called the Smiths?' He could see from Ma's face that the answer was yes. 'So are all those Smith children my cousins?' Did he want cousins? Cousins who already didn't like him? Bill almost shouted at Ma, 'Why didn't you ever tell me about them before?'

Ma flinched. 'Because, love . . . Well, I thought I'd never need to have any more to do with that family, that's why. Let's leave it at that, shall we?' Ma raised a finger to Bill. 'And I'd like you to keep away from them all, Billy.'

'But they're your family! *My* family!' Bill crossed his arms. Then he remembered the paper-spitting boy chasing him and throwing mud at him. Perhaps Ma was right. Maybe it was best to keep away from them all.

That night, Bill lay in his bed under the cottage thatch that rustled with mice, and his mind was equally busy with thoughts. Dad's job. That Smith boy. Thirteen Smiths in the village. Bill could feel his life shifting around him, and he didn't know how it was going to settle. He did want change. He wanted to leave school and earn money and explore the world. But he didn't want the change of Dad losing his job. He didn't want Ma upset as well as unwell. Was there a way he could make sure that Dad was the one Mr Widnall kept on? He smiled in the dark, thinking that, perhaps, there might be.

Chapter Three

'Can I help at Mr Widnall's this morning?' Bill asked Dad, as they shared hot oatmeal and cups of tea.

'You're not to miss a school day,' said Dad. 'Education –'

'– is important if I want to find a position of work that makes Ma proud, I know,' sighed Bill. He hated the idea of sitting at a ledger in a bank, adding up sums and writing neat copperplate lines; it would be just like school but for longer days and for ever and ever, all while wearing a stiff collar. That was Ma's dream, not his. 'But school doesn't start till nine, so there's time, isn't there? I can fetch things for you.' With his bad foot, Dad found carrying hard. He spent much of his time standing still at the benches in the greenhouses, planting and dividing his dahlia plants. He even talked to them. As if the plants were babies in a nursery. Bill supposed that's why the job was called being a 'nurseryman'. Dad sometimes sang while he worked. *I wish I could be a gardener like Dad,* thought Bill. *But perhaps one who travels to collect new plants from foreign places.*

'Well, it's true I've a lot to do to prepare for the flower show,' said Dad. 'You're a goodun, Billy boy, to help me.'

I'm helping me too, thought Bill. Out loud, Bill said, 'Think how proud Ma will be if you win that prize.' Inside he was thinking, *If Dad wins the prize for Mr Widnall, then Mr Widnall couldn't take away his job, could he?* 'Come on then, Dad.' Bill cleared the bowls and pan into the wash bucket, and reached for his jacket.

The morning was chill and damp, with a rosy tinge to the misty haze as the sun rose up the sky behind it. *All things bright and beautiful,* thought Bill, remembering the Harvest Service in the church a couple of weeks before. There had been wheat and apples displayed on the church window sills, along with some of Mr Widnall's dahlias.

Some of the village homes they passed were no more than sagging wattle-and-daub hovels built of sticks and mud and tatty straw, yet the morning light picked out spots of coloured flowers among the cabbages in their gardens, which truly were bright and beautiful.

What else did that hymn say? *The rich man in his castle, The poor man at his gate, God made them high and lowly, And ordered their estate. Well,* thought Bill, *rich Mr Widnall not only lived in a good brick house that was three storeys high and handsome, he had built a strange sort of pretend tumble-down brick castle in his garden.* A 'folly', he called it. Daft, in Bill's opinion. Why use good building materials and skilled workmen to build something with deliberately broken walls, so that it wouldn't even keep the weather out? If Bill could ever afford a castle, he'd want a proper one. But gentlemen's minds seemed to work differently from ordinary people's.

Dad opened the gate to the area where Mr Widnall's greenhouses were. *The poor man at the rich man's gate,* mused Bill. But Bill's family wasn't poor. They had more than most people in the village. Bill had good stout boots. Ma had a pottery dog and pretty plates on a dresser, along with a fine thin floral cup and saucer she was proud of. They had meat to eat every Sunday. But if Dad lost his job, what then?

'Carry this, would you, Billy?' said Dad, handing Bill a heavy watering can from under the water butt.

'Did you know they're expanding the coprolite mining?' said Bill, watching Dad's face.

'Are they?' Dad chuckled. 'It's amazing the money to be got for a load of old stones.'

So he doesn't yet know about the flower fields going, thought Bill. 'Are coprolites just stones, then?' he said, heaving the watering can through the greenhouse doorway and onto a bench.

'Well, they are and they aren't.' Dad was poking gentle fingers through the leaves of young dahlias, searching for flower buds and pests. 'It was a load of coprolite nodules, collected as ordinary stones to fill holes in a road, that started the whole digging them up and making manure of them a business. Ooh, here's one.' Dad made a face as he pulled a wriggling earwig from a bud. He nodded towards a pile of newspapers. 'Tear a bit of that paper, Bill. Give it a twist to make a little bag, then we'll pinch out any more earwigs in the blooms.'

'Who found out that coprolites weren't ordinary stones then?' said Bill, tearing and twisting the paper.

'A farmer over east of here,' said Dad. 'They were taking a load of Suffolk Crag they'd dug to mend holes in the road, and a cart wheel went right into one of the holes, upending the cart and tipping the stones into a corner of a field.'

'What's Suffolk Crag?' asked Bill.

'Just a load of rubble, really. They call it nodules. Nodules or coprolites or fossils. Why they can't settle on one name, I don't know. Anyway, the men with the upturned cart, they cleared up the spilled mess, but they can't have done a complete job because the dust from the bottom of the cart couldn't be got up from the soil.

Next summer, what do you think? The turnips in that corner of the field came up bigger and better than any in the rest of the field. They worked out it must have been the nodule dust that did that to the turnips in that corner.' Dad was carefully watering the dish beneath each dahlia pot. 'University and church sorts of educated men have studied the stones since then, and they say that the nodules are fossils. Bits of plants and even bits of animals, all mashed up and turned to stone. You know that bag of feed that we sometimes use to enrich the soil? That's made from grinding old bones and blood. Well, the nodules do the same job, apparently, so now farmers fertilize the soil with ground-up fossil nodules that they call manure.' Dad set down the watering can. 'D'you remember that piece of coal, Bill?'

Last winter Bill had earned some pennies from old Mrs Widnall by splitting her good coal. Ordinary, rough, coal was used to heat the greenhouses and Bill's home, but expensive, good coal that didn't smoke was used for the Widnalls' indoor fireplaces. The shiny, good coal came in big chunks, and if you tapped them with a point-headed hammer in the right place, the chunk would split neatly in two. When Dad was showing Bill how to do that, the very first piece of coal Bill split revealed something wonderful inside it.

'A fern,' Dad had said. 'Well, I'm blowed!' They'd

tilted the coal in the light, to see the imprint of fern more clearly. 'See that curly end to the leaf? Just the same as the fern leaves in Mr Widnall's terrarium.'

'What are those spotty bits on the leaves?' Bill had asked.

'Spores,' said Dad. 'Strange plants, ferns. No flowers on them, so they can't make seeds. They have these spores instead.' Dad rubbed his chin. 'Makes you think, doesn't it? How long ago must that leaf have been lying there, to turn into coal? Must go back even beyond the time of Noah's Ark, I'd say. Some say that there were plants in the world before there were ever creatures or people. You show that fern to Mrs Widnall when you go for your penny, Bill.'

'How fascinating!' Mrs Widnall had said. 'And beautiful. Mr Widnall will be most interested in that. Thank you, William.' She'd given Bill an extra penny for the fossil, on top of the penny for his work. Bill would rather have kept the fossil himself and not had the penny, but he wasn't given the choice.

Thinking of that now, Bill asked Dad, 'How can soft bits of animals and plants turn to stone?'

'It's a puzzle, isn't it?' said Dad. 'But then water can turn into a sort of stone, and that's just as surprising.'

'Ice,' said Bill. He loved the way he and Dad didn't have to tell the whole of something to understand each other. They both loved chasing ideas further and further, through twists and turns, until they sometimes caught them, like a dog after a hare. But there was never any great hurry to their chase. Bill loved Ma, of course, but he thought about things differently from her. He often felt the odd one out in school, too. But Dad and he understood each other comfortably.

'Water can disappear into air on a hot day, so then it turns into a gas, very different from solid ice,' said Dad. 'This world is a wondrous place, Billy. And God's made it all just so on purpose, you can be sure, even if we don't understand it all yet.'

'Are you using fossil manure on these dahlias?' Bill was working along the staked plants in rows of pots, pinching out any earwigs he could find in their flowers. 'If you do use the nodule stuff, then the dahlias would be eating creatures! Carnivores!'

Dad chortled. 'I haven't tried it yet, but I might. Make sure you get every one of those blighters off the blooms, Bill. They hide, you know, and will eat the petals.' Dad used tweezers to gently pick out an earwig from deep inside a just-opening maroon bud of flower. 'This one's Widnall's Granta,' he said. 'Can you remember that? It'll have cupped petals. It's named after our river here, of course, although why that colour should make anybody think of the river I've no idea. These are special specimens, grown for the show.

They were first bred and named by old Mr Widnall, so our young Mr Widnall is particularly keen that they should win the prize for best six matching blooms.'

'And what about the best single dahlia bloom, which you are in charge of?' said Bill.

'Ah, I've got some beautiful King of Dahlias – again, bred by old Mr Widnall. There's a bud I've got my eye on for the bloom to display on Saturday. Come and see,' said Dad, putting down the watering can and hobbling over to another greenhouse.

The King of Dahlias flowers where white, edged in rose pink. *They are beautiful*, thought Bill, *but are they special enough to win that prize? Other people might have new sorts of dahlias to show, and Dad's job might depend on his flower winning.*

'What if you could make the flower blue?' said Bill.

Dad laughed. 'There's never been a blue dahlia yet,' he said. 'And you certainly couldn't breed a new colour in the few days we have before Saturday. That's a job that would take years of work.'

'Well, I know how to make it blue really quickly,' said Bill. 'You put ink in its water.'

'Really?' Dad stopped still and looked intently at Bill.

'Truly,' said Bill. 'I've done it with a daisy.'

'Well, I never! A blue dahlia! There's never been such a thing in all the years that the Widnall family have worked with these flowers.' He stopped still, looked sharply at Bill, and stroked his chin. 'I wonder . . .'

Chapter Four

Bill had to run from the greenhouses to squash into his place in the hot, cramped schoolroom, just as the morning bell stopped ringing. It felt as though the bodies and the walls were pushing in on him from all sides – even into his head, pushing out his thoughts of flowers and fossils and nature. Bill sat on the hard bench and looked ahead. There was the paper-spitting boy, who turned and glared back at him. Did that boy know that they were cousins?

'Alfred Smith, turn around and face the front!' said Miss Snelling.

So he's an Alf, thought Bill. *Alfred Smith.* Now they both knew each other's names.

At lunchtime, Alf and his brothers and sisters surrounded Bill outside.

'Billy Ellwood!' they said, as if it was the most

ridiculous name in the world.

'It's Bill,' said Bill. Ma and Dad called him Billy, but he didn't like others calling him that. The Smith children realized that as soon as he'd said it, of course, and used it all the more.

'Billy Ellwood! Silly Billy Ellwood! Smelly silly Billy!'

Bill knew that he didn't smell as bad as those grubby Smith children did. He knew that 'Bill', and even 'Billy', were good names. And yet the Smith children had the power to make him feel smelly and silly, and the children who had been Bill's friends his whole life were suddenly keeping their distance from him.

'Silly Billy wears frilly pantaloons!' said a small Smith boy. 'His family all have fr–'

'But *you're* part of my family!' said Bill, thinking that would shut them up. But it just made their faces turn fierce and spit at him. *So they do know,* thought Bill. *They think I'm grander than them. They're jealous.*

They snatched his apple, tossed it between them, then ate it, taking turns to crunch a bite of it in his face.

No wonder Ma hates them, thought Bill. *I do too.*

Old Mrs Coddle was at the house when Bill got home from school. She was dressed in her habitual tatty black dress, with a tired grubby-grey cotton bonnet hugging around her white hair and her narrow-mouthed face. She was on hands and knees, on the brick floor. She had a basin of water in which Ma's feet looked very pink and naked. Ma, sitting in a chair, tugged off her shawl and dropped it over her feet as Bill came in.

'The boy's seen feet before, I should think!' chuckled Mrs Coddle, and she moved the shawl away and went on rubbing Ma's feet.

'Are you bad again, Ma?' asked Bill. Ma had been ill so many times over the years, Bill was used to it. It was her legs swelling up that made her feel ill. That's why the doctor said she should avoid standing up.

'I can't fit my boots on any more,' said Ma.

'It's her feet, that's what,' said Mrs Coddle, holding a table leg and hauling herself awkwardly up onto her own feet. 'All swelled up and needing a vinegar soak. It's what you expect when –'

'Bill, can you fetch Mrs Coddle some of that damson jam I made?' said Ma. 'You'd like a pot of that, wouldn't you, Mrs Coddle? And then I mustn't keep you any longer.'

But Mrs Coddle had sat herself down on Dad's chair to get her breath back after the effort of getting herself up from the floor.

'I remember, Billy, a baby born with feet you wouldn't believe,' she said.

Mrs Coddle had delivered babies and cared for the

sick and dying in the village for years and years, and she always seemed to have a story of a kind you didn't know whether to believe or not.

'Go on, tell us about the baby's feet, Mrs Coddle,' said Bill, hoping that she and Ma would both forget about that jam. It was his favourite, and Mrs Coddle was always getting bottles and jars of things off people.

'Well, this baby, poor little mite, he had, ooh, now let me think now.' Mrs Coddle counted on her fingers. 'The usual five toes on each foot, I remember, but then one more toe coming out at the side. Same on both feet. Work of the devil, some said.'

'The jam's on the shelf to the right of the pickle jars,' said Ma, nodding at Bill to go and fetch it. 'You like jam on a milk pudding, don't you, Mrs Coddle? Billy will fetch it for you. Go on, Billy.'

But Mrs Coddle wasn't to be distracted. 'Although why the devil would bother himself with giving a babe extra toes, I can't imagine. But then I'm not a vicar.' Mrs Coddle chuckled. 'Others said those extra toes was good luck. But there's no more sense in that, is there? Where's the luck in having to pay more for shoes to be made special to fit around more toes? Tell me that!'

Ma was giving Bill a firm look, so he went to the jam shelf in the back place. He picked the smallest jar of jam from the shelf, and brought it for Mrs Coddle.

'Thank you, Billy,' she said. She grinned her toothless grin at him and patted his arm. 'I remember when you was a baby, you know. You –'

'Now then, Mrs Coddle,' said Ma, lifting her feet from the bowl, and struggling to stand up.

'No, Sally girl, don't you move!' said Mrs Coddle, heaving herself up from the chair. 'You let that vinegar soak out the swelling, then get Billy here to pour that water onto the rubbish heap, and the swelling will be thrown away with it, you'll see.'

Did pain really seep out into vinegar water? wondered Bill. He thought how the swim in the river had seemed to soak the fear and anger out of him the day before. Maybe it could. He wanted to ask Ma about her illness and understand it more, but not while Mrs Coddle was here.

'Hand Mrs Coddle her stick, would you, Billy?' said Ma.

'D'you know what I did about those extra baby toes I was telling about, Billy?' said Mrs Coddle, taking her stick. Bill shook his head, and he carried the jar of jam to the door as bait to lure her to go that way. 'I tied button thread tight around each of those extra toes where they grew off each foot. Tied it tight so's the blood stopped going into them. Then those little toes just withered to tiny twiggy things, and, a few days later, they fell off.' Mrs Coddle laughed. 'A dog got one toe and ate it before the mother could stop him!'

'Oh, gracious! You really must be on your way now, Mrs Coddle,' said Ma. 'Billy has things to do.'

'That dog died soon after, but whether that was on account of the devil's toe —'

'Bye, Mrs Coddle,' said Bill, and he shut the door on her.

'She's been here all afternoon!' sighed Ma. 'I don't think I could bear any more stories of her babies gone wrong. Now then, how was school Billy?'

'A waste of time,' said Bill. 'What's the point of labelling pictures of flowers, when I know more about them than Miss Snelling or the books do because I've got Dad telling and showing me things on real flowers? Can't I leave school now? I'm almost twelve, and maybe I can earn money to help with your being poorly.'

'No,' said Ma. 'You learn numbers and writing, Billy, and you can get a nice, steady office place of work, and never you mind about me. I'll be well again in due course.' Ma rolled a stocking ready to pull it over a swollen foot.

'But I don't want a job in a —'

'Turn away while I put my stockings on, please.' Ma straightened up with a wince. 'You certainly aren't going to leave schooling before Lily's children do!'

'I'm ahead of every one of them who's there, even the ones who are older than me,' said Bill. 'Some of those

Smiths don't even go to school.'

'Oh.' Ma sounded pleased. 'Well, I expect they've all missed some schooling over the years.'

'Why?' asked Bill. If he knew more about the Smiths, he might be able to defend himself against them better.

'Lil's my own sister, I know,' said Ma, shaking down her long brown skirt to cover her ankles, 'but that family are rough, Billy. Rough. Fred's been in and out of work faster than a wash being dunked in soapy water. Work of all kinds too, from what I've heard. Just whatever he can get, and it always ends badly. They're not steady, Billy, and that's the truth of it. My William, your dad, Billy, he *is* steady.' She sniffed again. 'I chose well and Lil chose badly. That's all there is to it.'

Was that all there was to it? Bill tried to feel smugly superior about the hoard of Smith children, who were 'rough', but he couldn't help feeling envious of them. They all had each other, as well as a ma and dad. He wasn't even sure he wanted to be 'steady'.

As the week went on, there were fewer Smiths at school. First it was the oldest girl, Lizzie, who dropped out.

'She's helping Mam with the washing,' was what Alf told Miss Snelling. Then the two oldest boys, Eddy and George, stopped coming. 'Working at the diggings with our Pa,' said Alf.

Lucky things, thought Bill. They'd be getting paid wages. They were out in the open, listening to the men's talk, instead of learning chunks of Bible or the names of rivers around the world. What was the point in being able to name them, if you were never going to see them?

In school, the youngest Smith children soon got bored of Bill when he learned to ignore them. They busied themselves with new friends or with playing games between themselves.

By Thursday it was only Alf whose eyes were still constantly watching Bill. Bill had overheard a conversation between Ted Dilley and Alf at lunchtime, with Ted asking Alf how old he was. Eleven, is what he'd said, with a glare that dared Ted to say that he was small and that he was low down the class for his age.

Does Alf hate me because he minds that I'm ahead of him? wondered Bill as he met Alf's glare, and for the first time he felt a bit sorry for his cousin.

'Alfred Smith, eyes front, please!' said Miss Snelling, cane in hand. 'Tell me, Alfred, what is twelve divided by three and multiplied by four?'

There was a long silence. Bill felt an echo of his own agony when Miss Snelling had wanted him to repeat what she'd said, and he couldn't. He heard other children sniggering at Alf's discomfort, just as they had at his. He should be enjoying Alf's turn with this torture, but he wasn't. Without really thinking it through, Bill found himself tapping on the desk, just loud enough for Alf to hear: one tap, a pause, then six taps in a row.

'Is it sixteen, Miss?' said Alf.

'It is. Good boy, Alfred,' said Miss Snelling, and the tension in the room subsided as attention moved off Alf.

As they came out of school, Lizzie Smith was there with some of the little Smith girls.

'Billy boy!' she shouted at Bill. 'Billy, Billy, B–'

'Stop it, Lizzie!' said Alf. And she did.

On Friday morning, Bill did a half grin to Alf as he slipped into school late, and Alf gave him a full smirk of a smile back before Miss Snelling told him to face the front. It was a relief.

Now, thought Bill, if only Dad could win that dahlia prize and keep his job, and if Ma could get properly well, then he could concentrate on working his way to the freedom of life as a gardener.

Chapter Five

That evening, when Dad came home from work, Bill was out the back of the house, greasing their best boots with a rag. Dad, smiling, stepped out of the back door and put a finger to his lips, checking over his shoulder before pulling the door softly closed.

'I've done it!' said Dad, rubbing his hands together. 'I've left some of my best blooms in water with ink, and they're turning a beautiful blue. It's a marvel! I feel like a magician!'

'I told you they would!' said Bill, throwing down the greasy rag and standing up, wiping his hands on his trousers in a way that would make Ma cross. 'Can one of them win that prize, do you think? Have you shown the flowers to Mr Widnall?'

'Not yet. Mr and Mrs Widnall are busy with guests who are staying for the show. Besides, I want to surprise Mr Widnall with it when it's on display, looking fine, in the show. He's a great man for trying new things, is Mr Widnall. He'll be pleased, I'm sure of it. Oh, this is a proud moment, Bill. The first blue dahlias! And I owe it to you.'

'I bet it does win!' said Bill. *And then your job will be safe,* he thought.

'I'm going to surprise Ma with it on the day too, so don't say anything to her,' whispered Dad as they headed inside.

But they didn't need to say anything to Ma for her to know that something was going on. As she served up potatoes and onion sauce she said, 'Well, you two seem fit to burst with something, and I'm supposing it's to do with the show tomorrow. Am I right?'

Dad went a tell-tale bright red. 'We just might have a surprise for you, Sal. If I win the money, I'm going to buy you the cloth for a new dress. How about that? What colour would you like?'

Then Bill and Dad both said 'Blue?', together, and burst into giggles.

Ma looked from one to the other, and sighed. 'Well, I suppose I'm content to wait and see what this is all about,' said Ma. 'I'll have to be, won't I?'

They were all up before dawn the next day. Dad went straight off to Widnall's to pack the show blooms into the cart while Ma dressed in her best sprigged muslin dress over hot layers of petticoats. *I'm glad I'm not a girl,* thought Bill, although Ma was making him wear a collar that felt uncomfortably tight around his neck.

'Bill, can you come and stitch me into this bodice at the back?' said Ma. 'A button's come off, and I've no time for proper repairs. Oh dear, it's an age since I've worn this. Does it smell musty to you? It's had lavender bags around it to keep the moths off.'

Bill did his best with the needle and thread Ma handed him, but grimaced at the wonky stitching.

'Wear your best shawl on top, Ma, and nobody will see my sewing.' He smoothed his own hair down with water, and put on his cap.

'I did wonder whether my legs would let me go this year,' said Ma, looking in the small mirror on the bedroom wall, and tucking plaited ropes of her hair into loops around her ears. 'Can you see that I'm wearing your dad's second-best boots instead of my own ones? Tell me truly, Billy, because I won't go if I look a sight.'

'The boots are hidden under your skirt,' Bill reassured her. 'And who'd be looking at your feet anyway, when there'll be all those flowers and people to see?' *Why did Ma mind about such silly things all the time?*

Bill's tummy rumbled as he and Ma packed boiled eggs, pork pie, apples and lemonade into a basket that would ride with Ma on the cart. Lunchtime was a long way off.

'When we get there, can I go and look in the tents on my own?' said Bill. He wanted to see the flowers, but he also wanted to see the gardeners, in case there were any who might want an apprentice. He knew that Ma would mostly want to look at the gentry.

'Just so long as you don't do anything to disgrace me,' said Ma, reaching out to adjust his cap. 'I want to be proud of you.'

Mr Widnall's cart, with Dad in it, stopped at the cottage to collect Ma and the lunch basket, but there wasn't room for Bill. *Good,* he thought, and the moment the cart moved away Bill took the cap off his head, loosened his collar, and set off at a run, to make his way to Cambridge over the meadows.

Bill was used to Parker's Piece being a big, flat, green space, but now there were vast white marquees pinned down by guy ropes, there was bunting fluttering and music playing, dogs barking, children shouting, and people everywhere. He had to step aside whenever a grand lady in a fashionably large hooped skirt was coming the other way. There were men in suits of checkered cloth, in tail coats and tall stove pipe hats, and all sorts. All were dressed in their best. *Ma will love looking at all the flowers and feathers in the hats and bonnets,* Bill thought. He didn't need to feel guilty that he wasn't going to hurry straight to find her.

Bill went into the first marquee he came to. It seemed as big as Ely Cathedral. Would he spot Dad in here? There were flowers. So many flowers! Flowers were displayed on racks of shelving, but you couldn't see the shelves under the waterfalls of blooms tumbling from high to low. Mauves and yellows and pinks and whites. And the smells! *Yes, this is the world I want to be part of,* thought Bill. He looked under and around to spot the wire frames and the tubes carrying water and the coloured cloths behind displays – all the tricks to make the very best display of nature possible. But where were the dahlias? Where were Ma and Dad?

Bill found that the dahlias had a tent to themselves. In that tent were displays of dahlias in individual pots, dahlias cut and in vases, and dahlias built into fantasy scenery of magical hills or snowscapes of flower heads with model cottages in them. And on the central table at the back were vases holding the Best Single Bloom dahlias. Bill scanned the whites and mauves and oranges and pinks and yellows and reds, looking for a blue one. And there it was! It had a certificate placed beside it. And Dad was there too, beaming with pride.

'Look, Billy!' said Dad, pointing. The certificate beside the blue dahlia said, *Widnall's Blue Wonder, First Prize*.

'You won!' said Bill, and he felt his own mouth stretching wide in a smile that must have looked the same as Dad's. He saw now that Ma was sitting on a chair just to one side. She was smiling too, with tears on her cheeks that she was dabbing at with her handkerchief.

'Well, it's Mr Widnall who has won,' said Dad. 'I haven't seen him since the award was made, but the young and old Mrs Widnalls both said they thought the bloom a true wonder, and thanked me for it. Now Bill, could you take your ma and buy her a lick of ice cream? I must stay and speak to the other nurserymen, you understand, but the two of you should see all you can of the show and enjoy the treats to be had.'

As Bill helped Ma up off her seat, Dad caught hold of Bill's sleeve. 'Bill, lad, thank you for your idea. You're a bright one for plants. I could have a word with the growers here today and see if there might be a job going for you when you finish school. Maybe one of the colleges, or even one of the big London parks, would train you up. A grand place such as those might just sway your ma to agreeing to it. No promises, mind.'

'Oh, please, yes!' said Bill.

Bill found a bench for Ma by the bandstand. The stand fluttered with Union Jacks, and a brass band in uniform played jolly tunes. Bill and Ma had a penny lick each of rich, cold ice-cream that made Bill close his eyes just so that he could savour the sweet creamy vanilla flavour to the full.

'Life is good sometimes, Bill.' Ma smiled. 'And this is a golden day.' Bill didn't want to spoil the moment by mentioning gardening apprenticeships, but it felt just then as though his dream job might be possible – and soon. Meanwhile this last summer sunshine was to be relished, along with Dad's win and his own part in that.

Everything was as right as it could be with that day, until the evening. They were happily, tiredly, eating a supper of soup and bread, when a knock came at their cottage door.

Chapter Six

Bang, bang, bang!

That was the sound of a stick rather than knuckles on the door; a stick with a metal top to it, so it must belong to a gentleman, thought Bill.

'Whoever . . . ?' said Dad, rising from his chair.

'Ellwood!' yelled a voice from outside.

'That's Mr Widnall!' said Dad, reaching out to open the door. 'I wonder . . . Oh!'

Mr Widnall, frock coated, with his top hat in one hand and silver-topped cane in the other, stood on the doorstep, along with two other gentlemen. Mr Widnall's woolly side-whiskers were quivering with rage.

'How could you do such a thing, Ellwood?' Mr Widnall glared at Dad. 'You've made a perfect fool out of me in the most public of ways! You've made a mockery of the name of Widnall in the world of dahlias!'

'But how, Mr Widnall?' said Dad, his hands raised.

It was one of the other gentlemen who replied. 'It became clear that deception had been used to create the prized blue bloom, and so we have withdrawn that prize from Mr Widnall. He tells us that the colour had nothing to do with him, but was your trickery alone.'

'Trickery?' said Dad.

'No, it was *my idea*!' said Bill, pushing in front of Dad, but nobody was listening to him. Mr Widnall looked over Bill's head to wag a finger at Dad in the same way that Miss Snelling wagged a finger at naughty boys in school.

'You cheated, Ellwood!' Widnall went on. 'These two gentlemen here are judges from the show. They came home with me to see the Widnall's Blue Wonder growing – and I found white flowers, a pot of ink, and some stems in inky water with blooms turning blue.'

'Well, that *is* how I made the flowers blue,' said Dad. Bill saw that he was shaking. 'But I read the rules over carefully, and there is nothing there against colouring the blooms. You did say, sir, that I should do whatever I could to produce winning blooms.'

'Are you blaming *me* for this?' shouted Mr Widnall. 'Gracious, Ellwood, I thought you a better man than that. Of course colouring blooms falsely against their natural colour is the antithesis of what plant breeding is about. That is so obvious that it doesn't need stating in the rules!' Mr Widnall shook his head. 'This makes me sad, Ellwood. You've been with my family for a good number of years, and up until now you have been an exemplary worker. But I can't retain a man who cheats, most especially when he puts *me* into a position of appearing a cheat. You are to leave my employ, Ellwood. Collect your things tomorrow and be gone.'

Then the three gentlemen left, leaving Bill, Ma and Dad simply staring at each other in silence.

Chapter Seven

It was the disgrace that crushed them.

'How will I ever show my face again in the village?' said Ma, pale and shaking. 'Mrs Buckle – oh, and Lil! How they'll be laughing at me!'

In the days that followed, Dad said very little, but sat with a look of astonished despair on his face. It was as if he couldn't move or do anything, now that his job had been taken from him. Bill still had to go to school. He heard the children's gossip at lunchtimes, picked up from the adults. They all talked of William Ellwood as a cheat.

'It wasn't him, it was me,' Bill told them, but nobody listened. Except, perhaps, for Alf.

'My dad's been in trouble before,' he told Bill one day, as they waited for the afternoon bell. 'And he's a good man, really. Don't listen to any of them. I don't.'

By the end of the week, Dad still seemed to be frozen and unable to do anything.

'I'll try again telling Mr Widnall that using ink was my idea,' Bill told him on Saturday. 'Mr Widnall was so very angry when he called with those judge gentlemen after the show that I don't think he properly heard me say it before. When he understands, he'll give you your job back.'

Dad looked up and shook his head. 'It'll do no good, Bill. I had a visit from Jim Ballard earlier. He told me that Mr Widnall is laying men off in any case. Stopping the flower growing because he's losing the big field to coprolite mining. Ballard says that Mr Widnall is looking for reasons to let men go, and I've gone and given him a plump ripe reason, ready for the picking.'

'*You* haven't, William!' said Ma, spitting out the words as she fiercely stirred something in a pan on the range. 'Billy's right that it's his fault. I thought I'd brought him up to know right from wrong! I thought I'd done enough!' Ma's face closed tight and she gave Bill such a look that he couldn't take being there a moment longer. He ran from the house, slamming the door behind him.

Ma hates me, he thought as he ran up the dusty street. *I hate me too.*

Bill ran down the road past the Bugs Row cottages where cosy candlelight flickered in the Smiths' small window. He ran past the church looming up in the darkness. Then he ran up the drive into the farmyard of Manor Farm where he could see Mr Lilley's old dog Rex tied by a rope.

'Rex,' called Bill, and he held a hand for the dog to sniff, then stroked around his ears. But a whickering sound from the small field drew him over to the gate to reach up to the large-headed carthorse. 'Hello, Dolly,' said Bill, recognizing her. 'I've done something bad, Doll. Have you ever done something bad?' The horse snorted warm breath on him, nodding her head and making him laugh a bit. 'No, you haven't,' he said. 'You're nice, you are. Not like me.'

Bill fed Dolly grass that he pulled up and held out on the flat palm of his hand, and he stroked and stroked down her hard, strong neck, and then her velvety whiskered nose. The horse gave a sympathetic nudge of her nose to Bill's armpit, and there was something comforting about her large strength and seemingly listening ears.

'You're a goodun,' said Bill, and tears came into his eyes. Dad wouldn't call him a goodun now. Bill leaned against Dolly's big head. He had no idea how long he cried, but his thoughts changed as he wept away some of his despair. Crying seemed to get rid of some of the hateful muddle inside him, leaving room for a determination to put things right.

Bill crept into the house very late. He lifted the latch as quietly as possible, and stole up the stairs.

'That you, Bill?' whispered Dad's voice from the big bed where Ma was sleeping.

'You're not asleep?' said Bill. He couldn't see Dad's face in the darkness. 'I'm sorry – sorry for all of it, Dad.'

'I'm sorry too,' said Dad quietly. 'Now go to bed, son.'

Ma was too unwell to go to church the next day, but Bill and Dad went, faces set firm as the village people looked at them and whispered. Bill sat in the back pew beside Dad, and watched the Widnalls walk up to their front pew. They were smiling and chatting. Bill had known Mr Widnall and his ladies his whole life. Dad had worked for them for years and years more than that. They were odd and gentry, but nice, he'd always thought. Bill glanced at Dad. He was looking at his hands in his lap, looking beaten. All because of Bill's idea that was never meant to hurt anybody, least of all Mr Widnall. A hot coal of anger smouldered in Bill throughout that church service. By the end of it, that anger was flaming. He and Dad left their pew as soon as the service ended, and Dad hobbled with his stick towards home.

'I forgot my cap, Dad,' said Bill. 'I'll just go back and fetch it.' Bill waited for Mr Widnall, together with his ladies in their big skirts, coming through the church door and shaking the vicar's hand.

'Mr Widnall, sir! Please, sir!' said Bill.

Mr Widnall sighed, gesturing the ladies to go ahead without him.

'What is it, William? I simply can't give your father his job back, you know.'

'But it was *my* fault, not his, sir! It was my idea to make the flowers blue with ink. My father didn't think of it.'

'Well, it was a clever trick, I grant you that much,' said Mr Widnall, smiling. Then his face turned hard. 'But you surely understood that it was cheating, plain and simple, and that it would therefore have serious repercussions? You are not a stupid boy, so I must suppose that you are a wicked one.'

Bill felt sick. Wicked? It hadn't felt wicked at the time. Could wickedness happen when you are trying for goodness?

Mr Widnall was still talking. 'Of course I feel sorry for your father, and for your mother who I gather is unwell just now, but I can't possibly employ the man who has embarrassed me within the dahlia world.'

'Could you give my father a letter of recommendation, though, sir? To help him get another job?'

'And say what in it? That I had to dismiss the man for making a public cheat of me?' Mr Widnall raised his eyebrows, replaced his hat firmly onto his head, turned his back on Bill, and walked off towards his house. Bill watched him go as a flurry of wind blew leaves across the church path. Winter was on its way, and its chill damped the fire in Bill's belly to ash.

Chapter Eight

The days that followed were grim. The weather was cooling, the days shortening, and money tight. Lunch had become a bowl of oatmeal, the same as breakfast.

'I'm saving the last of the tea leaves in case we have company,' said Ma. 'I've used the old ones again. There's little flavour left in them. Ouch!' She flinched as she set the pot on the table.

'Sit down, Sal,' said Dad, taking the pot from her, and pouring out what looked like clear hot water. 'I'll go tomorrow for a job at the diggings. They'll be taking on more men as they start the new fields. Then you can put your feet up and drink tea all day long.'

Bill noticed that neither of his parents even smiled at that little joke.

When Bill came home from school the next day, Ma was

knitting and Dad was sitting in his chair, doing nothing. No job.

'Did they say no because of my ink trick?' said Bill.

Dad shook his head. 'No,' he said. 'That didn't bother them.'

'What, then?'

'They said that the diggings was no place for a cripple.'

Ma looked hard at Bill, as if Dad being a cripple was his fault as well as the ink business. Bill said nothing. There was nothing to say. It was true that a man who hobbled as he walked and couldn't stand straight wouldn't be as fast at digging as a man with two good legs. The farms didn't want a lame labourer either. What could such a man do, even if he was the best dahlia man in the village?

In the following days, Dad took his stick and walked the neighbouring villages and into Cambridge, knocking on college and farm and house doors, asking for work, but finding none.

Bill, pausing unseen on the stairs one Saturday, listened to his parents talking.

'Without a reference, nobody will consider me for a full-time place,' said Dad. 'And even for casual work they all want fit and able men. Who can blame them?'

'That Mr Widnall!' began Ma, chopping beans. *Bang-bang* went the knife on the block. But Dad wouldn't let even Ma say a word against Mr Widnall.

'No, Sal. Remember that Mr Widnall's father took me on when I was a boy, despite my foot, and he trained me over the years. The fact is that I let the Widnall family down, and there's no getting away from that.'

'But I've been thinking . . .' Ma had stopped chopping. 'William, maybe you could set up on your own dahlia nursery? Just a small one?' she said. "William Ellwood and Son, Quality Dahlias." Doesn't that sound good?'

Bill bit on a finger and froze still to hear more. That idea certainly sounded good to him!

'That would be nice, all right,' said Dad. 'But I can't buy land and greenhouses and all without money, and . . .'

' . . . and Billy's lost you your job so there *is* no money for it,' said Ma, chopping fiercely again.

Bill swallowed back hard, clomping down the last stair and into the room.

'I don't want to be "And Son" anyway,' he said to Dad, but with eyes flashing at Ma. 'I want to do my own things!' And he slammed outside.

Dad's allotment meant they could still have some vegetables. Dad took to setting out to the allotment each morning as if it was his job, and Bill joined him when he could, to help with lifting and carrying.

'Jim Ballard has given me early beans to get in,' said Dad. 'That'll be something to harvest once spring comes around. And I can maybe sell some of these cabbages.'

But three weeks after Dad lost his job, he came home, kicked off his boots at the back door, and didn't place them neatly side by side as he usually did.

'That's it, then,' he said to Ma and Bill. 'I can't grow us anything more than will fit in that patch beside the hens at the back of this place. They've taken my allotment from me.'

'They can't do that!' said Bill.

'They just have,' said Dad.

Ma put her head in her hands.

'Why?' said Bill.

'Because the allotment rules state that no unemployed man is allowed to work allotment land,' said Dad.

'But that's our food they're taking from us!' said Ma. 'Those committee men were your friends, William. Your friends!'

'That's why they say I can harvest what there is on my patch before it's handed on to the next man.'

'Oh, very kind I'm sure!' huffed Ma. 'I suppose we save the rent on it.'

Dad sighed. 'Rent's due on this place at the end of the month.' He shook his head. 'I don't know what to do about it.'

Bill had never heard his father use those words before. Dad always had one idea or another to make things right.

It frightened him. So did the look on Dad's face. Bill had never seen a grown man cry, and especially not his dad.

'Let me work!' said Bill. 'I want to!'

But Ma wagged a finger. 'Billy, if you can't be part of a family business with your name over the door, you need to work for others, and for that work to be nice work. I've kept you at school to raise you into being a gentleman. Don't you take that from me, too. I'll see if Mrs Foulkes might give *me* some work again,' she said. 'If I have to do it in your father's boots, then so be it. The village can laugh some more at me, and I'll have to weather it. You just make sure to learn all you can at school, Billy. *That's* your job, young man.'

Bill tried to concentrate on doing the sums and copying the lines of dull history neatly onto his slate to somehow make amends to Ma. But he knew that this work wasn't turning him into the gentleman she longed him to become. In fact, being at school seemed to work the other way. It was making him a thief.

'You know this village, so where's the best place for scrumping?' asked Alf one lunch break. Bill had never scrumped apples before, but he'd heard other children talking about it. So Bill and Alf sneaked off after school to steal apples from the vicarage garden and from the Widnall's. From up in the tree's branches, you could look over to the Widnall's house and see the maid bringing in the washing. Straight from the tree, the late season apples tasted sweet. 'They won't catch us,' said Alf. 'If they notice anything, just throw an apple over that way, and they'll look there while we nick off.'

Bill enjoyed the thrill of knowing they might get seen. It was fun doing it together with Alf. *I'm already wicked,* he thought, *where's the harm in adding to the list of my sins?*

Ma lasted just three days of working for old Mrs Foulkes. She had only been doing light jobs such as dusting because Mrs Foulkes knew that Ma wasn't well. But on the third day up at Wrights Farm, Ma fainted, hitting her head as she fell. Dad was called to fetch her home, and word came to Bill in school.

'Your mam's in a bad way, Bill!' Alf told him. 'Our Lizzie saw her being took home from Wrights' Farm when she went to fetch the washing. Your mam was all white and shaky and had blood on her head, Lizzie said.'

Bill ran out of school, straight home, not caring that there'd be a caning for it later. 'Ma?' he said, bursting into the house.

'Get back to school, Billy,' she said. 'I'm all right.' But she didn't say it in her usual, fierce way. And Dad looked really worried.

'I'm caring for her,' said Dad to Bill. 'You go.'

Bill went, but to the Widnall's orchard on his own to steal apples.

Even kind Mrs Foulkes couldn't employ Ma when she was like that, but Mrs Foulkes did give Ma some sewing jobs to do at home. So, when Bill got home again at the time that should have been after school, Ma was sitting with her feet on a cushion as she grimly hemmed big white sheets with stitch after stitch. Dad had Ma's pinny on and was clattering pots in the sink in the back place. Bill stood for a moment and looked at them.

Everything is all wrong, he thought.

'Have an apple, Ma,' he said, taking a good one from his pocket.

'And where did that come from?' said Ma sharply. Bill said nothing. Ma sniffed, and jabbed her needle into the sheet hem. 'You've stolen it, I suppose?' She didn't take the apple.

Ma was paid two shillings for her work, which paid off the bread and butcher and milk bills, but didn't help towards paying the rent. Ma was hardly eating now, for all that her legs and belly were swollen.

'You've got to eat and keep your strength up, Sal,' Dad told her. 'I'll see if the chickens have laid you an egg. That would be nice, eh? Soft boiled and easy to eat?' And he went out to the chickens at the back.

How much food did a body need to keep strong? wondered

Bill, as he swept out the hearth and set the new fire ready. Fires ate wood or coal . . . or a whole house or a village or a town if they got the chance. Miss Snelling had been telling them about the Great Fire of London. But you had to get fires going with little dry bits of twig, and then grow them with bigger stuff. What might work as kindling to Ma's appetite? Wasn't it calves' foot jelly and beef tea for ill people?

'Doesn't Mrs Buckle bring food for people in the parish who are poorly?' said Bill. 'In that basket of hers with the cloth over it? Why has she stopped coming here to see you, just when she might be useful?'

'A lady such as Mrs Buckle is not going to associate with a family of thieves and cheats,' said Ma stonily.

So somehow that was Bill's fault as well. Well, if the church turned its back on you, surely family would stick by you in hard times?

'What about Auntie Lil, though, Ma? Shall I ask her to come and see you?' said Bill.

Ma reared up out of her chair. 'Don't you dare, Billy Ellwood! I've told you to have nothing to do with those Smiths.' The wobble in her voice stopped Bill from asking what he longed to know. Why did Ma think the Smiths so awful? He was getting to like Alf, and even the other Smith children were sometimes friendly towards him now. He'd seen their mam, his Auntie Lil, in the village, skinny and tired looking, but with a smile for all those children she had. Bill could see that Lil was Ma's sister. They had the same wide mouths, but they used those mouths in different ways. Ma hadn't smiled her mouth at Bill for a long time.

So, thought Billy, *Ma won't ask family for help. Dad can't find work. Ma is too ill to work. Rent for the house has to be paid. Winter is coming. I've got to work, whatever Ma thinks,* Bill decided, as he walked to school.

Out of the Smith family, only Alf and three younger brothers were there in the schoolroom now. The bigger boys were working as barrow boys at the diggings, earning good wages.

Bill took a seat on the bench next to Alf and whispered, 'Your dad and brothers work at the coprolite diggings, don't they? Have they got any more jobs going for boys, do you know?'

'Dunno, but I'll ask if you like,' said Alf. 'You have to be older than us to be a barrow boy, though. Sixteen before you can be a digger. They're the ones who really earn well.' Alf paused, then said, 'You can come to ours at lunch break if you like. Then we can ask my dad.'

Bill knew exactly what Ma would say about that invitation. But, thought Bill, she wouldn't be surprised that he wasn't doing what she wanted him to. She expected him to be bad, so why not be? He felt excited at the prospect of going inside the Smith home, meeting them all. *Is this what it feels like to be wicked?* he wondered. If it was, he quite liked it.

'Yes please then, if that'll be all right with your mother,' said Bill.

'One more or less won't make no difference in our house,' said Alf.

Alf's mother did look startled, but then pleased, to see Bill coming into her house.

'Oh!' she said. 'You're Billy, aren't you? Billy Ellwood?'

'Yes.'

'Well then, call me Auntie Lil, love,' she said. 'I can't give you more than bread and scrape, but I'll make a brew of tea since you're company. Your Uncle Fred'll be here soon for his lunch.' Auntie Lil looked Bill properly in the face, and smiled wide. She reached over and touched Bill's head. 'You're a tall lad, Billy – taller than our Alf.'

'Mam!' said Alf. 'Leave him be!'

'Sit down then, Billy,' said Auntie Lil. A crowd of Smith faces looked at Bill from around the table and all around the room. It felt more like being in the schoolroom than home to Billy. He wanted them to all stop looking at him.

There weren't enough chairs for them all. The little ones sat on the steps. Not enough cups either, so they shared. Bill, as a guest, was given a cup and seat to himself.

He wondered whose place he was sitting in.

'Don't you take more than your share!' said Alf as Bill reached into the tangle of arms and hands grabbing at the pieces of bread and scrape on a big cracked platter. Bill took a small bit, which he ate slowly, making it last. The others all got talking, louder and louder as they tried to be heard above the others. Bill liked the fact that they soon lost interest in him, and he could hide in their crowd and laughter. Only Auntie Lil seemed to be still watching him whenever he glanced her way.

'All right?' shouted Alf in his ear, and Bill nodded. He thought of his own neat, quiet home, and how he hadn't heard laughter there since the day of the flower show. It must be nice having brothers and sisters, he thought, even though some of them were rough-and-tumble fighting on the floor now. *That's what Ma doesn't like,* he thought. *It's because they don't pretend to be almost gentry, like she does.*

When Uncle Fred came in, tall and dark and angular, the one downstairs room of the cottage was even fuller. Fred stooped to come in through the door, blocking the slight light that came through the window from outside, so that the room became almost dark. Bill stood up to let Fred have the chair.

'Hello there,' said Fred, sitting down. 'Who's this, then?'

'That's your nephew,' said Auntie Lil. 'William Ellwood. Billy.'

'Is it, now? How's your parents, Billy?' said Fred. 'I heard that your father had a bit of bad luck.' He chortled. 'I heard that he made a fool of that Widnall fellow! I've seen Mr Widnall lording it over people. It's about time somebody brought him down a peg or two! *Well done, William Ellwood,* I thought when I heard what your dad had done. I'd never have thought William had it in him to play a trick like that with Mr Widnall's precious flowers!'

'He didn't . . . Well, never mind.' Bill bit his lip. 'Mr Smith – I mean, Uncle Fred – are there any jobs for boys going at the diggings just now, do you know?'

'They're after a horse boy, I know that,' said Fred, taking a tin mug of tea from his wife, and sitting down. 'Timothy Pawley broke his leg falling out of a tree yesterday, so he's no use for some weeks while it mends. I told Mr Gander who runs things that our Alf might suit the job. Do you want it, Alfie?'

'What's a horse boy?' said Alf.

'You know that big round business where they wash the nodules, ready for carting?' said Fred. 'Well, somebody's needed to walk the horse round to power the washer.'

'I could do that,' said Bill.

'Dad said it's my job!' said Alf. 'You find another job, Billy Ellwood!' And suddenly Alf was climbing over his small siblings, making for the door.

Bill grabbed Alf's sleeve to hold him back. 'I *need* that job!' said Bill, bolting for outside as well. 'I really do.'

Fred Smith laughed as the two boys shoved through and out of the door. Then they were running hard towards the diggings field.

Bill ran without caring whether or not he could breathe, whether his legs hurt or not. He just ran as fast and true as possible, very aware of smaller wiry Alf right beside him. Alf suddenly cut a corner, ducking down beneath Bill's arms to get in front. Bill grabbed hold of Alf's shirt, feeling it rip as he ran to get past him again. They arrived at the field together, out of breath, shouting and waving their arms to try to get attention.

'Mr Gander! Here I am! Horse boy job!' panted Alf.

'Give the job to me!' said Bill, pointing at himself as he bent over, catching his breath. 'Please.'

'Please, sir, me!' Alf was jumping up and down.

Mr Gander and the other men were sat on planks, finishing their lunches, and they laughed at the boys, just as Fred Smith had done.

'Well,' said Mr Gander. 'I can see that you're both very keen, and both fit enough to run, so that's good. But I'm not interested in who wants the job the most. I want to know who can do the best job with the horse.'

'I can!' said Alfie, his hand flapping in the air as if he

was in school. 'I helped Mr Dykes with his milk round when we lived in Ipswich! I was always at the brewery stables too, helping.'

Bill felt hollow with disappointment. How could he fight Alf for the job, when he didn't have any experience with horses? All he'd done were small jobs washing flowerpots and splitting coal for the Widnalls, and Mr Widnall certainly wasn't going to give him a good reference.

'I've put harnesses on horses, and fed them and brushed them and everything!' Alfie was up and down in front of Mr Gander like a flea.

'That's all as maybe.' Mr Gander got to his feet. 'But it's Dolly who will know which of you two she can work best with.'

Dolly! Bill felt a small flicker of hope.

'Who's Dolly?' asked Alf.

'The horse in question,' said Mr Gander. 'Over there.'

Large and cloppy, shaggily grey-coated and wise-eyed, Dolly was tied to the fence, munching grass. She lifted her big head as Mr Gander and the boys came towards her.

'Well, Dolly,' said Mr Gander. 'What do you think of these two lads, eh?'

Dolly clopped a big-hoofed step towards Bill, and butted him gently with her long face. Bill smiled and stroked down Dolly's nose.

'Oi, Dolly, do you want some nice grass?' said Alf, elbowing at Bill, and offering a handful he'd pulled up.

But Dolly didn't even look his way. She shoved her nose under Bill's arm to lift it, prompting him to reach up to pat and stroke her strong, hard neck again as he had done that night after the flower show.

'Well, that's it, then,' laughed Mr Gander. 'Bill, is it? You can start right away if that's agreeable to your parents. You'll be paid six shillings at the end of each week, if you prove satisfactory.'

Bill felt something that had been solid inside him melting a little. No more school. A job with a horse. Money for Dad and Ma!

'But that's not fair!' said Alf.

Mr Gander shrugged. 'That's life, son. Sometimes it falls your way, sometimes not.'

Alf turned on Bill, shouting into his face in a way that made Dolly tense and back away. 'You only knew about the job because of me!'

Bill wasn't surprised when Alf jumped on him, hitting and hitting as they wrestled together, cheered on by the watching men. Bill fought to save himself, but not to hurt Alf. Alf was right, after all. Bill would be furious if he were Alf. But this job might save Bill's family, so he wasn't sorry. With his longer arms, he could hold Alf so that his punches failed to hit, but that made Alf even angrier, until he untangled himself and ran off home.

Bill watched him go. *I've lost a friend,* he thought, *but at least I've got a job.*

Chapter Nine

Bill soon got used to the new pattern of work. He woke each morning, as he always had, when the six o'clock church bell rang, dressed quickly, and climbed down through Ma and Dad's bedroom to the room below, where he'd eat a bowl of hot oatmeal before hurrying outside. Dad made him the oatmeal each morning now. He'd taken to doing Bill's jobs at home, as well as Ma's and his own. He'd say to Bill, 'You get off. I'll do the chickens and the other chores. You're the earning man these days.'

It felt good to be the earning man, but Bill hated to see the look of defeat in Dad's eyes. And he hated, hated, hated the way Ma looked so disappointed in him, when she could bear to look at him at all. She spent much of her time in bed now, bundled in shawls and a patchwork quilt. *She's keeping away from me,* thought Bill. Dad was always taking her bowls of food, to try to tempt her to eat, and Mrs Coddle still came to soak her swollen feet, even though there was no jam spare to give her in return for that now.

'She comes for a gossip as much as for anything else,' Dad told Bill. 'I get out of the house and help Jim with his allotment when she comes. Jim gives me the odd cabbage in return.'

But once he was at the diggings, Bill could forget about home. Each morning he had to collect Dolly from her small field at Manor Farm. He'd pick a handful of the longer grass outside the field, then open the gate and go in, clicking his tongue against his teeth to call her. She'd lift her big head at the sound from him, nod it up and down, and then amble over. That was pleasing. She always chose to come to him, even though she knew it was in order to be harnessed for work.

'You're a goodun,' Bill told her, slapping her warm, dusty neck and letting her munch the grass and dandelion leaves from his flattened hand. Then he'd slip the rope halter over her head and lead her through the gate and over to the digging field and the washpit, ready to work the machine.

The diggers, washer men and the barrow boys, their trousers tied below the knee with string lally lags, would gather first thing in the morning for the day's work orders from Mr Gander. Their shirts and jackets and boots and trousers were all already a ghost-like grubby white from the clay dust. Soon their faces and hair and hands would be covered in it too. That dust and mud was another thing Ma sniffed at about Bill's work. She'd make Bill take off his boots and jacket before letting him into even the back scullery, then wipe a cloth over anything he touched. He stripped and had a cold wash in the scullery sink before she'd let him into the main room. It was Dad who washed the clothes now, hanging them over the wooden clothes horse to dry in the last warmth from the fire overnight.

As Bill stood looking at the other workers, he noticed some of the men wore bright red kerchiefs at their necks. Those were clean at the start of the day, adding one bright bit of colour. Bill would have liked to have a kerchief like that.

Some of the diggers and boys were from Grantchester, and Bill already knew them. Others came from villages round about, and there were some Irishmen who'd come from work digging railway cuttings. Those navvies were the best trench diggers in the coprolite fields, and they knew it. They lived in lodgings at one of the pubs or in houses that had spare rooms to rent. Most of them drank hard in the evenings and at weekends. Ma sniffed at that hard drinking too. Dad wouldn't have liked working amongst those men, thought Bill, although he might have enjoyed hearing their wild stories of railway building. Uncle Fred fitted right in, sometimes drinking his wages away on a Saturday, so that Auntie Lil was known to ask the parish relief fund for bread and coal. Bill's family hadn't done that yet, and Bill knew it would wound Ma's pride even further if it ever came to it. It did seem to give her a grim satisfaction when, in the evenings, Bill sometimes told of Fred's misdemeanours.

'I told you, Billy, there's no steadiness in that man.' Ma would tut. But, steady or not, Fred was earning more for his family than Dad was just now. So was Bill. And he was enjoying doing it. The work was laborious and repetitive, but it had interest. The earth wasn't, as he'd supposed, the same as you went down through it. Grantchester had a clay soil. Dad had shown Bill how compost could add acid to that alkaline clay soil to let azaleas grow. Bill knew that other places had sandy or peaty soil. But he hadn't known the variety to be found in the layers below the topsoil on any one spot. Now he looked down into trenches dug eight feet deep, and he saw stripes of knobbly gravel, white chalk, and grey smooth clay, as well as the thick brown topsoil of the fields.

'Why are there those different layers?' Bill asked the men working the trench.

'What does it matter why?' they said.

So Bill asked Mr Gander. Mr Gander stroked his chin. 'It's a puzzle isn't it, Bill? They say there's millions of years between some of those layers. Millions.'

'But who is "they"?' said Bill.

'The surveyor chap, for one,' said Mr Gander.

The nodule digging was done in trenches cut in lines over the fields. A surveyor gentleman would visit and use a metal screw bore to cut down through the earth for samples, finding where layers of coprolites might be found. They'd peg and string out a line for the men to cut in places that looked promising. When that trench had been dug out, and the nodules taken from it, they'd fill the trench in again and another trench would be dug beside it, building a striped pattern of pale, chalky lines of used trenches across the field.

'Those diggers should be putting the top soil back on top,' said Dad, when Bill told him about it. They were eating a stew for Sunday lunch, and even Ma was tasting some of it. The meat had been bought with part of Bill's first handful of pay, and it tasted especially good to him because he'd earned it. 'Those fields won't grow their crops well if it's chalk or gravel they leave on the surface,' said Dad. But, meanwhile, the coprolite mining was earning more for the landowners than crops ever had.

Bill's job wasn't in the trenches where the coprolites were hacked out, lifted in buckets, and then wheelbarrowed over planks to the washmill. The washmill was where Bill and Dolly worked, along with some women who shovelled the stones in and out. The washmill cleaned the nodules, ready to be sold to the fertiliser mills.

The washmill itself was a mound with a sort of dry moat around it. Bill and Dolly walked around and around that moat, pulling a metal arm that turned a post at the centre of the mill to pull water up and into the mill. The slurry waste from that washing was channelled away, and the cleaned nodules were loaded into carts. Bill sometimes helped the women to pick the ordinary stones from the nodule pile. Only true coprolites could be turned into fertiliser. Bill soon learned how to recognize the coprolite nodules among the stones. They were black and knobbly. Mr Gander said that coprolites came out white in other places he'd worked. Why was that? wondered Bill. But people came in black or white too and yet were the same inside – according to Dad, who'd once met a black man – so why not stones, too? Mr Gander showed Bill a final test to do on a stone, to be absolutely sure that it was a coprolite.

'Strike it against something hard, just as you would a flint against a firesteel. If you smell sulphur, that's a nodule. If not, it's an ordinary stone and needs throwing onto the pile for road-building rubble,' he said.

There was the constant sound of machinery grinding,

water sluicing, and workmen grumbling and laughing and shouting as they went about their tasks. Bill and Dolly plodded round and round, always turning right, into shade and out into the sunlight if it was a fine day, constantly wet and cold if it was a rainy day, always longing to unwind in the other direction. But Bill could escape into his thoughts even as his feet went over and over the same ground. He thought of how the earth goes around the sun, and how he was on the earth, which was going around itself as well as around the sun. He thought of the seasons going around because somehow time was going around as well as objects going around. It made him dizzy to think of it all.

About three weeks into his job, when Bill sat to eat his lunch of bread and cheese with the others, he asked, 'Those nodules or coprolites or whatever you want to call them, are they really fossils and bits of animals? They don't look it to me.'

'I reckon nodules are bits of the moon,' said one man. 'That's what they look like. They broke off the moon and landed here, hundreds, maybe even thousands, of years ago, and that's why they're so deep down in the soil now.'

'Well, that's nonsense, and you know it!' Mr Gander told the man. 'Don't listen to him, Bill. The nodules are bits of animal and plant and whatnot turned to stone. We've had university men down here taking an interest, telling us to keep an eye out for anything that looks particular, and they'll pay money for any fossils they can use.'

'Use for what?' said Bill. 'How much do they pay?'

'Blowed if I know what they want them for,' said Mr Gander. 'Especially since the gentleman I spoke to told me that nodules were mostly made of . . . well, something that came *out* of animals, rather than the critters themselves.'

'Turds, you mean?' said Bill.

'That's it, but turds turned hard as stone, over time. They say that if you crack them open you might find seeds or bits of bone of whatever the animal had been eating.'

'But what sort of animal did the poo in the first place?' said Bill.

'Great, strange creatures that were too big to be saved on Noah's Ark when the flood came,' said Mr Gander. 'That flood was the end of them, and that's why they're called antediluvian creatures, meaning they were only about the place before that great flood.'

'Are there stone turds from people too?' said Bill.

Mr Gander snorted breadcrumbs from his mouthful of lunch. 'Lord, I hope not! Or I'm going to start wearing gloves when I work!'

'I don't think there were people on the world then,

were there?' said another man.

'What about Noah? And his family? And the wicked ones who drowned?' said Bill. 'How –'

'Oh, I don't know, lad. You'll have to ask one of those university gents. Or the vicar. They understand all that stuff. Our job is just to collect the blessed things, and we'd best get back to it, or we won't meet the quota and we won't get paid.' He folded the cloth his lunch had been in, and stood up from the plank.

After that, Bill noticed, picked out and kept interesting-looking nodules he found. There were pauses in the work, when the stones and nodules were cleared from the washpit and a new lot loaded, or when there was a blockage in the water pipe. Then, Bill would sift through the pile of nodules, and pick out anything that looked a definite shape. There were some that were a curled, horn sort of shape.

'Devil's toenails is what we call them ones,' he was told.

There were 'thunderbolts' too – long and thin with one spiky end. And Mr Gander showed Bill a curled, ridged nodule.

'Here's a fossil for you, Bill,' he said. 'You can have that.'

'Oh yes,' said Mrs Coddle when Bill showed that particular one at home. She was there with Ma again. 'Those curly stones are petrified snakes. Saint Patrick turned all the snakes to stone, and that's one of them. Carry it in your pocket and it'll bring good luck, Billy.' She handed it back to him. 'D'you know, that shape reminds me of the ear of one of my babies I brought into the world. It had one ear that was like yours or mine, Billy, but the other one was all fat and curled around and squashed. The little mite had held its ear in its fist inside the mother. That mother would sing so, and all of a screech like a jackdaw, so you can't blame the babe for holding its ear. Or was that ear cursed? I never . . .' And on she went.

'Take that thing outside, Billy,' said Ma. 'We've enough going wrong already without you bringing in ungodly bits and pieces.'

'Why do you say it's ungodly?' said Bill.

'Why do you question everything?' said Ma. 'Just take that thing out, and take it right out!' said Ma, angry at him again.

So Bill escaped out the back, where Dad was mending the chicken run in the dusk. *Dad's keeping out of Mrs Coddle's way,* thought Bill.

'D'you believe that Saint Patrick made snakes into stones?' Bill asked him, showing the fossil.

'That looks more like a sea creature to me than a snake,' said Dad, turning it and peering at it. 'Snakes don't have those ridges round them, do they? At least none that I've seen in pictures or heard of. Nor the grass snakes we get around here.'

'But how can it be a sea creature? We're miles and miles from the sea,' said Bill.

'This world's a strange old place, once you start noticing,' said Dad. He straightened up, awkward in his lopsidedness. 'And, um, I'm going to see a bit more of it as it happens.' Dad handed the fossil back to Bill. 'I've got work.'

'Really? Is it gardening? Why does the work mean you'll see more of the world?' Bill felt a stab of jealousy at that thought, even though it was good to see Dad smiling.

'It *is* gardening, but it's away from here. I haven't dared tell your mother yet.' Dad took off his cap, ran a hand through his hair, then placed the cap back on. 'I don't want Ma upset, but she's got to be told. I'll be working at a grand house and estate, Audley End, over twenty miles away, I'm told, so I'm to live in. Jim Ballard gave my name to a man looking for a dahlia breeder, so that was good of him. I'm to teach the gardeners there all about dahlias so that they're prepared when the new season comes around.'

'How long will you be away?' asked Bill, biting his lip. Could he care for Ma on his own?

'Only a few weeks. I can't leave your mother as she is for too long.' Bill handed Dad's tools to him, one at a time. Dad wrapped them in a sack, ready to stow in the shed. Bill felt a bit sick at the thought of trying to humour Ma on his own. Maybe she'd forgive him for the loss of Dad's job, now that Dad had a new job. But maybe she'd want Bill to go back to school! Surely not, when Dad's new job was short term? Bill knew it was a wicked thought, but he was glad of it.

Dad was whistling as he shut the shed door. Bill hadn't heard Dad do that since he'd lost the job at Mr Widnall's. Bill took a deep breath. 'I'll look after Ma,' he said. 'I promise I will.'

Chapter Ten

'Stop!' said Mr Gander the next morning, as Bill was harnessing Dolly into her traces. The autumn mornings were chilly now, and Dolly's breath steamed. 'You're not working the washmill today, Bill. Neither you nor Dolly. The carter's horse has gone lame, so we need Dolly to help pull the load into town.'

'To the wharf?' said Bill. 'To the barges?'

'That's it,' said Mr Gander. 'Bring Dolly round to the loading bay.'

'Please, can I go too?' said Bill. He longed to see more than the trudge around the washmill. 'I can look after Dolly.' Bill had seen Silver Street wharf a few times when he'd walked into Cambridge with Dad. It was always busy with boats and hoists and carts and people, with the big, old beautiful buildings of Cambridge around and beyond it.

Mr Gander gave a curt nod. 'I tell you what, Bill, buy me a tin of baccy for my pipe while you're there, and I'll let you go.' Mr Gander handed over a little silver sixpence.

Bill helped to load the cart with the piles of clonky, washed nodules, and harnessed Dolly to the cart. He walked beside Dolly, up the road and out of the village, past the terrace of cottages and the big house at the end. Then they were in the open. The fields either side of the road had been ploughed into thin ridges, showing dark and light strips even though they were all the same soil. *Light and shade,* thought Bill.

'Get a move on, Bill,' said the carter. 'Give old Dolly a slap.'

'Come on, girl!' said Bill, but he didn't slap her. Dolly threw her weight into the harness, and heaved the load up the slight incline. At the top of the road, you could look across to King's College chapel's pale rows of turrets spiking the sky. Bill smiled to see it, remembering how Dad had once told him that King's College chapel gets called 'the upside-down pig' because the corner turrets looked like legs and the little ones looked like rows of teats. Through the village of Newnham, and then on into Cambridge, Dolly pulled the heavy cart. There was traffic in the town; horse-drawn cabs and carriages, men on horseback and on bikes. Bill, walking beside Dolly's head, almost forgot to steer her through it all as he took everything in, and was distracted by gownsmen hurrying by in their black gowns and with square, tassled mortar boards on their heads.

'Why do they wear those flat hats?' Bill asked the carter. 'Are they called mortar boards because of builders' mortar, for sticking walls together? What's mortar got to do with university men?'

The carter shook his head. 'Oi, steer Dolly over that way and watch out for that rut or we'll be into it.'

Over the bridge, across the river to Silver Street wharf, and they came to a queue of carts and wagons waiting their turn beside the barges. Sacks and barrels and crates of corn and coal were being offloaded from barges and onto carts, and nodules loaded into the barges to go the other way. It was a noisy muddle of the clatter of horses and shouts of men. Dolly's ears flicked back and forth, and she pawed a big hoof on the cobbles.

'Steady, Dolly,' said Bill. 'Hold still.'

One of those university men was at the wharf as the carter and Bill waited their turn for the nodules to be weighed and put onto a barge. The carter caught Bill's eye and nodded towards the young man in a black gown and mortar board.

'That young gent there with the side whiskers is Mr Seeley. He's one for studying fossils. I've heard that he's been known to pay as much as one and six for a good fossil stone.'

'I've got some snake stones,' said Bill. 'And loads of devil's toenails, and one thunderbolt. Look.' Bill pulled out the handfuls of stones that had been weighing down his pockets. 'D'you think he'd . . . ?'

'Nah.' The carter scrunched up his face. 'Those are too common for him. And that one's all broken, look. It's not even properly curled.' He pushed back the cap on his head. 'Fella on the market might take the whole ones. He polishes stones and sells them to gentry. Lord knows why they want them, but that's gentry for you. It's a market day today, as it happens.'

'Oh,' said Bill. 'Er, Mr Gander told me to buy tobacco for him while I was in town, so please might I . . . ?'

'Get off with you!' laughed the carter. 'You'd be more hindrance than help with the heavy work, in any case. Be back here before Great St Mary's Church clock strikes midday, if you want a lift back in the cart. If not, you make your own way home.'

'Thank you!' said Bill, giving Dolly's neck a parting pat. 'Be good, Doll.' Then he was off, weaving through the crowd of carts and people, up Mill Lane and towards the market. There was King's College chapel, huge and beautiful in the sunshine now that he was close to it, and not at all like an upside-down pig. Pale stone, carved and fancy, with great, grand windows that Dad said were painted by Dutchmen, hundreds of years ago. All fenced off from the street, of course. But there were shops with window displays – coloured glass bottles and boxes printed with pictures and words, a tailor sitting cross-legged in the light to stitch a jacket collar, and Bill smelled a wonderful mix of spices through one shop door. Then he was into the open market, and there were rows of stalls. Great St Mary's church stood on one side of the market square, so Bill would be sure to hear the hours chime. On the other sides of the square were the tall court house and rows of brick-faced shops.

In the middle of the cobbled square stood a grand water fountain. Bill scooped his hands to take a quick drink, then turned to look at the stalls roofed with tarpaulin and set out with sacks of grains and flour and meal, baskets of cabbages and potatoes, wet fish, cheeses and pies, and hanging, dead birds and cuts of meat. And there was the fossils stall. A man behind that stall was writing out labels with a tatty quill. On the stall there was a basket labelled with the word *ammonites* on a bit of paper with his scratchy, inky writing. Those ammonites were snake stones, realized Bill. Thunderbolts were labelled *belemnites*, and devil's toenails were something else complicated beginning with *'g'*. There were bigger fossils, displayed individually with labels and prices.

There were smooth, shiny spirals on slices of stone.

'Are those the insides of snake stones?' asked Bill, pointing.

'Oi, don't you touch anything you can't afford. Get off with you. Hop it!'

'I'm not buying, I'm selling,' said Bill. He pulled the snake stone and devil's toenails and one thunderbolt from his pocket and held them up for the man to see.

The man's mouth curled into a sneer. 'Common as muck, those.'

'But they're the same as what you've got in those baskets at sixpence a time,' said Bill. 'Wouldn't you give me a shilling for the lot of them? Please? There's nine of them, so that gives you a good profit.'

'*Profits*, is it? So you're a businessman, are you?' The man's fat finger poked at the fossils in Bill's hand. 'I'll give you tuppence for the lot.'

'That's not –' began Bill, but a gentlemanly voice from behind cleared its throat to get attention, then spoke.

'Young man, I *will* give you your shilling, but I only want the turrilite.'

Bill turned. Black gown billowing, Mr Seeley, the university gentleman from the wharf, stood there, pointing at one of Bill's fossils. 'That turrilite is something of a rarity, as this chap well knows.' Mr Seeley was looking at the market man with one eyebrow raised.

The market man went red. 'Ah, Mr Seeley, I, er, didn't see you there. I hadn't noticed that particular stone. The boy failed to point it out to me.'

'Because, as I am sure you were hoping, he had no idea of its value,' said Mr Seeley.

Bill looked at his fossils. The one that Mr Seeley was taking from his hands was the odd snake stone. It was chipped and you could only just see that it was a sort of short, fat, unicorn-horn shape, with the curl pulled upwards.

'What's good about that one?' said Bill.

'It's an example of something rather rarer than the usual ammonite,' said Mr Seeley. 'In fact, I want to know where it was found, if you could tell me.'

'In Grantchester. I took it out of the nodules being washed at the diggings there.'

'Ah, so you're in a position to look out for more interesting specimens, are you? I'd be happy to pay if you did find anything more of particular interest. My name is Seeley. I work for Professor Sedgwick.'

'I'm Bill, sir. Er, William Ellwood. Who is Professor Sedgwick, please?' said Bill. 'And how will I know if I have a fossil of a kind you want or not?'

'Professor Sedgwick is Professor of Geology, and a very great man who knows more than almost anybody about fossils. I could take you to see our museum, and then show you the kind of thing we're after, if that would suit?' said Mr Seeley. 'The museum is just beyond Great St Mary's there, so very close. Have you the time?'

'Oh! Yes!' Bill thought of the lift home in the cart that he would lose if he was late. But it wasn't so far to walk home. And this was a chance to see inside one of those great, huge university stone buildings.

When Bill saw the Cockerell Building rising in front of him, enormous, with grand pillars and leafy carvings in its smooth pale stone, he looked at his grubby hands, then wiped them on his trousers.

'Is *that* the museum, sir?' he said. 'They'll never let me in there!'

Chapter Eleven

Mr Seeley pulled open a big door to the museum, and stood to one side, nodding Bill to enter. 'The gentleman who put together most of this collection over a hundred years ago left instructions when he died. He said that his fossils and the rest of it should be free to be seen by 'all such curious and intelligent persons as shall desire a view of them for their information and instruction'. Isn't that marvellous? And you, I take it, are a curious and intelligent person?'

Bill certainly was curious, even if Miss Snelling might not agree about the second part, so he stepped inside . . . then stopped still.

'Oh!'

The long white room had arches down either side and had a rounded roof that seemed as high as the sky.

And there, standing in front of Bill and looking straight at him, was a big skeleton of a large creature with huge antlers. Bill laughed. The laugh echoed in the big space, and Bill clamped a hand to his mouth. Glancing around, he saw that there were much odder skeletons than that big deer thing, though. 'What very strange beasts,' said Bill.

'Come and see,' said Mr Seeley, smiling broadly. 'I think these will interest you.'

The museum had fossils from all over the world. Most exciting were the really big skeletons of dinosaurs. '*Dinos* meaning "terrible" and *saurus* meaning "lizard",' explained Mr Seeley. 'In Greek, of course.'

'That one doesn't look like a lizard,' said Bill, pointing to a huge case on the wall holding a skeleton as long as the cottage where Bill lived. The creature had a leaf-shaped body, a tail and four paddle arms. But strangest of all was its long swan-like neck.

'*Plesiosaurus Giganteus*. Found by Mary Anning,' said Mr Seeley.

'But that's a girl's name!'

'Yes. Miss Anning learnt to look for fossils when she was younger than you are. She lived on the south coast, at Lyme Regis. She collected and cleaned fossils to be sold to tourists. She and her father and brother made some remarkable finds.' Mr Seeley smiled. 'An exceptional woman, Mary Anning. She made something of a fool of the great Frenchman, Cuvier, who thought that he knew all there was to know about such creatures. When he saw this particular plesiosaurus here, he claimed that it was a fraud. He said that Mary Anning had put together bones from bits of different creatures. He was sure that no real creature could have that long a neck in comparison with body length. He declared that she had taken the head of a lizard, teeth of a crocodile, the bones of a snake for the neck, the trunk and legs of an elephant, and the paddles of a whale! Can you imagine? He was wrong. It was a creature that swam in and on the water, rather like a gigantic swan, using that long neck to plunge down to catch fish or reach vegetation.'

'Gracious!' said Bill, and knew he was sounding like his mother when she saw that he'd torn his jacket. He wanted to say so much more to express his wonder, but didn't have the words, so he just looked and listened. But Mr Seeley seemed to understand, and showed him more and more, though some of the exhibits on show were much smaller and duller than the big creatures.

'Those lumps there are like what we dig up,' Bill pointed out, surprised that those little nodules would be worth showing in such a grand place.

'That's right,' said Mr Seeley. 'Coprolites. The word coprolite comes from the Greek again, *kopros* meaning "dung", and *lithos* meaning "stone".'

'So Mr Gander was right when he said that they were turds!' said Bill.

Mr Seeley's finger went to his lips. 'Not so loud! It was Professor Buckland of Oxford who came up with the name "coprolite", when he found them within the fossil skeletons of some big ancient beasts. So, rather than being "turds", as you put it, they are as often food waste that's still in the digestion tubes as they are waste that's been excreted. But coprolites can also simply be a mish-mash of bits of bone and shell that's stuck together into a lump by the processes of time, and not passed through any creature at all.' Mr Seeley's hands were the most expressive Bill had ever seen, drawing in the air.

'But how could the bits and pieces get mixed up like that if they hadn't been eaten?'

'Because land doesn't stay still,' said Mr Seeley, moving on from that display case. 'It's becoming clear that our land has moved great distances over very great stretches of time, and that movement has stirred things somewhat. Look at this.' Mr Seeley led Bill towards a table which had drawings laid out on it. The drawings showed layers of land, some of them rippled, some folded. 'This is what earth looks like if you cut down through it. Have you seen cliffs at the seaside? Or observed mountains where there has been a rock fall?'

'No,' said Bill. 'But the trenches at the diggings have stripes of different soil at different levels, just like in those drawings. I'd like to see cliffs, though.'

'When you do you'll notice how the land can be layered, and how those layers fold, almost as if they were fabric, sometimes folding layers right over and under each other. Water moves things as well, dropping them in new places.'

'It does that in the river,' said Bill. 'I've seen. The river puts bigger stones on one side of a bend and little stones and sand on the other.'

'That's an excellent observation,' said Mr Seeley. 'You see, you *are* that intelligent and curious sort of person the Woodwardian Museum is meant for!' He said this quite loudly, and Bill suddenly realized that he was saying it partly because a number of gowned gentlemen had gone past them, looking disapprovingly towards Bill.

'But none of that would have brought sea creatures all the way to Grantchester, would it? We're too far from the sea to visit in a day, my dad says.'

Mr Seeley smiled and raised his hands. 'But Grantchester certainly was *under* the sea at some point in the past. The fossils you've collected yourself prove that. Sea creatures in abundance. You may never have been to the sea, Bill, but the sea has been to you.'

Bill's eyes opened wide. 'When?'

'That's the big question,' said Mr Seeley, shrugging and grinning. 'An extraordinarily long time ago, that much is clear.'

'Were there people who saw the sea here?' said Bill. His voice was rising again, but he didn't even notice the stern looks being shot his way by gentlemen bent over desks, reading and writing. His mind was in a Grantchester under the sea. 'Did people live with the dinosaurs and big deers, and –'

'– rhinosaurus and a sort of hairy elephant called a woolly mammoth?' Mr Seeley smiled. 'Those creatures were in the Cambridge area too, you know. We've found fossilized bone shapes from both. But they lived here at quite different times from each other. The rhinoceros lived in a hot climate, the woolly mammoth in a cold climate. Neither of them when the sea was here, of course. It's all very complex and all very fascinating.'

Old Mrs Widnall had once shown Bill a big book of animals while Mr Widnall and his father were talking about dahlias. There had been a picture of a rhinoceros in that. 'Rhinoceros. That's *saurus* again,' mused Bill. 'But they're not lizards. They live in Africa now, don't they?'

'Yes, hot Africa, thousands of miles away.'

'So how did they get from Africa to here?' said Bill.

'Let me show you a rather interesting map,' said Mr Seeley, and he tipped a large roll of paper out of a tube. The map that Mr Seeley unfurled onto a big table was a map of the world, like the one Miss Snelling had borrowed from the vicar and shown them in school one day. Mr Seeley used fossils to hold down each corner of the map. Then he took some paper shapes from a drawer.

'Are those countries?' guessed Bill.

'Continents,' said Mr Seeley. He placed the continent shapes over the same continent shapes on the map. 'Now, watch this.' Mr Seeley pushed South and North America across the Atlantic Ocean . . . to sit snugly against Africa and Europe.

'They fit each other!' said Bill, almost shouting in his excitement.

'They really do, don't they?' said Mr Seeley. 'Hardly a gap. The thought is that America and Europe and Africa must all have all been together as one enormous land in the distant past. Animals could roam anywhere on that huge land. Then parts of the land broke off and moved, taking animals, or their remains, with them. So Britain was part of Africa. That's quite a thought, isn't it?'

'Did Grantchester people eat rhinos, do you think? Did they live like African natives?' said Bill. Then he looked at his own hand. 'Why aren't I dark-skinned like Africans, then? Did we get pale when we went north and it got colder?'

Mr Seeley lowered his voice. 'Big questions, eh? And

we don't yet have all the answers. Actually, some scientists now suspect that man didn't even exist in those times.' Mr Seeley looked at Bill. 'After all, we don't find human fossils. In fact, when I was at the School of Mines I learned how the very deepest fossils being found in the coal mines show plants and some very odd fish-like things, but no animals at all, let alone humans. A Mr Charles Darwin, and others too, believe that life changed over millions of years, with humans arriving relatively late into the world. Things evolved over enormous stretches of time.'

'God can't have made the world for people, then,' said Bill. 'But if God made the world for dinosaurs, then why aren't they still around?'

'Shush!' Mr Seeley put a finger to his mouth again, and nodded his head towards where a white-haired gentleman in a clerical collar was frowning fiercely. 'Not everyone agrees with Mr Darwin's ideas, not even Professor Sedgwick. Come and see something more, and then I must get to my lunch, and I suspect you must do the same.'

Bill was fairly sure that he must have missed St Mary's chiming for midday, but he didn't mind that. He just wanted to see all that he could with this man who knew so much and who took his questions seriously.

Mr Seeley showed Bill some stuffed and bottled birds and creatures. 'See these ones?' Mr Seeley pointed to a case of small birds. 'These were brought back from his travels to the other side of the world by Mr Darwin. The fascinating thing he found was that these particular birds are not found anywhere on earth except in the Galapagos Islands. And there are some other creatures which are found only in Australia.'

'So those lands *weren't* ever joined to Africa?' said Bill.

'Seemingly not.'

'But why did any of the land move?' said Bill. 'Isn't it fixed with, oh, roots or something? Did God change his mind and move it about, or did it move on its own?'

Mr Seeley raised his hands. 'That question is exactly what scientists and men of the church are arguing about. Some think that God can't have made a mistake or changed his mind. Others think that the world, and its creatures, have changed and evolved over more time than you or I can get our brains to think about.'

'Mr Gander said that God killed off the dinosaurs when he made the Great Flood,' said Bill. 'The dinosaurs were too big to fit in the ark.' He frowned. 'But some of these old animals could swim, couldn't they? Do you think the dinosaurs were wicked, like the wicked people God was drowning with his flood, Mr Seeley? Why would God make wicked things in the first place? Why didn't he make people right, so that he didn't have to kill them?'

'So many questions! And I don't have the answers.'

Mr Seeley pulled out his pocket watch. 'Oh, Lord, I *am* late for lunch. Quick, let me just show you what I really brought you here for. I want you to see the kinds of fossil that I'd like you to look out for at your diggings.'

There was a large display case full of stone snakes and thunderbolts and devil's toenails labelled with ink lettering on paper stuck to them.

'I've never seen such big ones!' said Bill.

'Yes, all of these are particularly interesting examples for a number of reasons,' said Mr Seeley, and he quickly pointed out the kinds of examples Bill should look out for. Fossils imprinted with insects. Vertebrae from a creature's backbone. 'Or,' said Mr Seeley, 'maybe you could find me something that's never been found before. I have high hopes for you, Bill Ellwood! Now, you'd better get back to wherever you are supposed to be. You can find me here, or in my rooms in Sidney Sussex College if you do find anything of interest.'

Bill left the museum, with his head spinning full of ideas and thoughts. He ran back to the wharf well after midday, but luckily the carter had refreshed himself at the pub and was still there, so Bill got a ride back to Grantchester on the empty cart pulled by Dolly.

'You're very quiet,' said the carter. 'Run out of questions at last?'

Actually, Bill's head was so full of questions that he

didn't have space in it to think of anything else. It was full of the past and strange creatures and land that moved, and how some of the past was still here, as fossils. In fact, he had quite forgotten to buy Mr Gander's tobacco.

By the time he reached home, it was raining. The house was dark, with only the small flickering fire in the grate giving a little light to the room and glinting on Ma's damp cheeks.

'Ma?'

'Your father's gone to the railway station, off on his way to that job,' said Ma. 'Mr Ballard took him when he was going to the station to pick up a package, which was a kindness when he didn't have to. But if only Mr Widnall had found it in his heart to keep your father on in spite . . .'

So Bill had failed right from the start in looking after Ma for Dad. He'd missed Dad leaving by being so late home.

'I've got something for you, Ma. Hold out your hands.' Bill put the two sixpences and the collection of pennies and halfpennies and farthings he'd got for his fossils into Ma's thin hands, and folded her fingers over the money.

'But it's not pay day,' said Ma. 'Oh, Billy, you've not gone and st–'

'Stolen it? Is that what you think of me, Ma? I know

I'm bad, but I don't steal money. Mind you, I might as well if that's what you believe I am like!'

'Oh, Billy, I didn't mean to –' began Ma.

But Bill had already stormed off upstairs. He sat on his bed, missing Dad, and missing the Ma who used to think he was a good boy she was proud of. As he stared out of the window at grey clouds smudging the sky, the wonders he had seen and heard about in Cambridge seemed very distant, and suddenly unimportant after all.

Chapter Twelve

With Dad gone, Ma hardly able to glance at him without looking disgusted, and Alf not speaking to him since he'd got the job with Dolly, Bill was lonely. He longed for someone to talk to about what he'd seen and learned about fossils. And he longed to lift the guilt that he felt towards all three of those people. So, when he saw Alf bringing Uncle Fred's lunch over the field next day, he called out, 'Hey, Alf! D'you want to make some money?'

Alf pretended not to hear, so Bill ran over to intercept him on the path.

Alf looked the other way.

'I know how we can make money, working together,' said Bill.

Alf's steps slowed, and he frowned, but still didn't look at Bill.

'By selling fossils,' said Bill.

Then Alf did look at him. 'How? Who'd pay for those dirty old things?'

'Mr Seeley from the university,' said Bill. He grabbed Alf's sleeve to stop him. 'I got paid a shilling for one special fossil yesterday. The market stall man sells ordinary ones to gentry. We could do what he does, cleaning up fossils and selling them to gentry ourselves. I reckon, with two of us working at it, we could make lots of money.'

'And how do I know you won't pinch it all, like you pinched the job that was as good as mine?' said Alf.

Bill didn't know how to answer that, but the look on his face must have told Alf something because Alf laughed at him.

'Go on, then,' he said. 'How do we do it?'

'We find the fossils, clean them up, then put them in a basket. Then we go and find gents or ladies who seem to like them. Charge them a lot, and they'll think they must be special.'

'Are the gentry really as simple in the head as that?' said Alf.

'We'll find out, won't we?' said Bill. 'And I know what to look for that might be rare and special and worth more. Mr Seeley —'

'Off you go, young Smith,' Mr Gander interrupted, coming up to them. 'There's work to be done. And, Bill, I've not forgotten your failure to buy my tobacco. Get Dolly working quick-sharp or I might wonder if I was really right to hire you.'

All week Bill looked out for fossils. Alf came to the digging field before school and at lunchtimes, and together he and Bill searched the piles of nodules. Some of the diggers and washers began to look out for fossils for them too, after Bill told them things he'd learned from Mr Seeley.

Mr Gander let Bill keep the fossils in a corner of the shed at Manor Farm where the diggers ate their lunch when it was wet. One of the Irish navvies, Patrick O'Brien, began collecting fossils when he heard there was money to be made. All the Irishmen gave their finds to him, but the village men gave them to Bill and Alf. 'Here you are, Professor Ellwood, another of your stone thingamies!' they'd say.

'We need to clean the fossils,' said Bill, looking at the grubby pile with Alf one lunchtime. 'But my ma won't let me have fossils in the house. We could put them in a bucket out the back, but . . .' Bill tailed off because he was about to say that Ma wouldn't have a Smith in the house either, and maybe not even out the back, but he couldn't say that to Alf.

'Oh, come round to mine,' said Alf. 'Mam won't mind. She likes you.'

So, when work finished at noon on Saturday, Bill took the fourteen fossils wrapped in a bit of old sacking around to the Smiths' house on Bugs Row.

'What's he doing here?' said Lizzie. 'Didn't he take your job, Alf?' She was heating irons by the fire and using them on shirts that weren't properly dry, so the small cottage was steamy. She hardly had space to move her hot iron over the blanketed corner of the table because three other girls were sat on the chairs, busy with sewing, two of the boys were fighting on the floor, and baby Mops was sat by the step, grizzling and chewing on a wooden spoon. 'Teething,' said Lizzie, noticing Bill looking. 'Ain't nothing that will shut her up until that tooth comes through.'

Bill knelt down in front of the baby, and made a face that stretched his mouth big and eyes wide . . . and baby Mops stopped her noise and stared, then smiled a big gummy grin.

'Leave her be,' said Alf. 'We've got fossils to clean and money to make.'

Outside in the small yard, Alf took Auntie Lil's wash tub down from its nail. Bill tipped the fossils gently out of the sacking, clanking into the tub.

'They don't look anything special, do they?' said Alf. 'Who's going to want to buy them?'

'They'll look better when they're cleaned,' said Bill. They used water and scrubbing brushes to get the loose dirt off the fossils. They looked more appealing when they were done, but still like stones and not very special.

'Varnish is what they need to make them shine,' said Alf.

So, once the fossils had dried, they gave each one a wipe of varnish from the bottom of a tin begged from Mr Dilley, the joiner, down the row. The fossils did look smarter, if sticky. 'Got to let them dry again,' said Alf.

'I reckon we could sell some to the vicar,' said Bill. 'Dad said Reverend Buckle had a drawer full of fossils in his study. He saw it when he went to ask if Reverend Buckle could help him to find work.'

'Did the vicar get him work?' said Alf.

Billy shook his head. 'But Dad's got some work now anyway, away at a big house.'

'It would be for a *big* house, for you Ellwoods, wouldn't it?' said Alf. 'Have to be better than the rest of us, don't you?'

'No!' said Bill. 'It's only a temporary job. I don't know what he'll do after that. I bet your dad's job earns more, Alf, honest.' He turned the sticky fossils so that they could dry on all sides. 'We need the money from these things just like you do. For the doctor for Ma, for one thing.'

* * *

In the evening darkness after work and school on Monday, the two boys went selling. Bill had changed his mucky work trousers and jacket for his Sunday ones, and Alf had borrowed his brother Eddy's boots, so the two of them looked quite respectable as they stood shivering at the vicarage front door. The weather had turned really cold, threatening that winter wasn't far off.

The vicarage door was a big one under a porch with stone pillars. There was a handle to pull a chain out of the wall that rang a bell deep inside the house. Beside the door hung a fancy lantern, the metal cut in a pattern of ivy, with a lit wick flickering inside it. In the door was a brass letterbox mouth, waiting for packages and letters.

A maid opened the big door. It was Ena who'd been at school with Bill until last year. 'You can't come here!' she said, glancing over her shoulder. 'Go to the tradesmen's entrance.'

So they went around to the side of the house, to a door that didn't have posh stone pillars holding up a roof over you as you waited, or a lit lantern to welcome you, or a brass handle to pull and make a bell jangle somewhere inside. They knocked on the ordinary door, and it was still Ena who opened it.

'What've you got in there, then?' she said, poking at an ammonite in Alf's basket.

'Fossils,' said Bill. 'We thought the vicar –' But before he could say more, there was Mrs Buckle sweeping to fill the doorway with her great hooped tartan skirt.

'What do you boys want?' she asked tartly. Then she saw what they had in their basket, and her hand went to her throat. 'Oh no,' she said. 'Not fossils. From those awful diggings, I suppose. Well, I won't have those heathen things in *this* house, and neither will the vicar!'

She doesn't know about those fossils in his desk drawer, then, thought Bill. He supposed in a big house like this there was room for more secrets than would ever hide in his or Alf's sorts of home. But didn't God see all?

'Who is there, Mama?' asked one of the vicar's daughters, trying to push past her mother's skirt to see.

'Nobody at all,' said Mrs Buckle, and she slammed the door shut.

'Charming,' said Alf.

'She thinks fossils make people doubt that God made the world in six days, all of a piece and just how he wanted it,' said Bill, remembering what Mr Seeley had told him. 'She's right about that.'

'What are you on about?' said Alf. 'Oh, come on, I'm freezing! Let's try Mr Widnall and his ladies. They wouldn't take against fossils, would they?'

'I'd rather not see Mr Widnall,' said Bill. 'I don't think he'd buy off me.'

bit of a lump, then bigger, bigger, bigger, then pop! Out it comes, scraggly and bawling, and Ma's back to being as skinny as a rabbit ready for the pot. Until it all starts again, and then . . .'

Bill didn't want to hear more. He could only think of one thing: Ma's new baby would likely be a nice one. A good one to replace wicked Bill who was no good at anything.

Chapter Thirteen

Bill watched Ma when he got home. She was standing by the fireplace, one hand on the mantelshelf, her face pale as she prodded the fire with a poker. The room was chill in spite of the small fire. Bill could see the bump on Ma now that he looked for it. It was partly hidden under Ma's criss-crossed shawl, but still distinct on her skinny body. Ma saw him looking.

'Fetch in some more coal, will you, Billy?' she said, turning her back to him.

Bill didn't move. 'You're having a baby,' he said. 'Why didn't you tell me?'

Ma paused, stiff, then turned to face him. 'It's really nothing to do with you,' she said. 'Now, the coal.'

Nothing to do with him? 'That baby's what's making you ill, isn't it?' said Bill. 'Will you be better when it's born?'

'Coal,' said Ma.

Ma said nothing further on the matter when Bill brought in more coal, and he didn't dare ask more for fear of upsetting her. He'd promised Dad he'd look after her, after all. But thoughts of babies and fossils and dinosaurs swirled in Bill's head all evening. And in the night he woke from a dream in which a great lizard monster was licking at his forehead.

'Get off!' Bill sat up, thrashing his arms. In the complete darkness under the thatch, he couldn't tell where he was for a moment. Then – *splat!* A cold drop landed on his face. His arm was wet too. Dad's old shirt that Bill used as a nightshirt was damp down one side, cold and clammy. The thatch was leaking. There was no lizard monster. Bill could hear the rain now, pouring down on the thickness of straw. Bill was in bed, safe at home, so why did he still feel the patter of panic in his chest? Then he remembered.

The baby. The baby making Ma ill.

In the cold, damp darkness, Bill was afraid. Ma was getting more and more ill. He'd heard her being sick yesterday evening. Yet she hadn't eaten anything all day. That couldn't be right, could it? Pregnant ladies had to eat to keep themselves strong to grow the baby. The bump showed that the baby was growing, so was it taking all the goodness from what little food Ma did eat, leaving none for her? What if Ma died?

Now that Bill thought about it, he realized that Ma must have had babies inside when she was ill those other times. He'd never see a baby; just sadness in his parents. So those other babies must have died before they were ready to be born. Where were those dead babies now? There were no graves for them in the churchyard.

Bill thought of Mrs Coddle's stories of babies being born dead. What if this one got born dead too? Bill suddenly *did* want a brother or sister. And of course Ma *must* get well again! He loved her, for all that they fought sometimes.

Bill felt sick. How could he make the baby live this time, when he didn't know anything about babies and women and all that, and he just seemed to upset Ma all the time?

That's why Mrs Coddle is around so much, he realized. But did grubby old Mrs Coddle, with her stories of babies gone wrong, really know how to make it all work right? She clearly hadn't with any of Ma's other babies. Except for the baby that was him, of course.

Bill hugged himself. The baby inside Ma now depended on Ma being kept warm and fed and happy. No wages had arrived from Dad yet.

Bill threw back his covers and got out of bed. He dressed in the dark, crept downstairs to get pots and a bucket, and carried them back up to put under the worst leaks through the roof. Stealing past sleeping Ma, he was very aware of a small baby sibling within her under the covers.

Bill was too awake to think of going back to bed once he'd sorted the leaks, so he did the morning chores around the house, prodding the fire back to life, putting the kettle onto the hob, going out to see that the chickens were surviving the weather. What could he do to make things better for Ma and the baby? If only it wasn't so windy, if only it wasn't a Sunday, he could have knocked on doors and offered to rake up leaves for a little money. Then he thought how there would be nobody around to see and disapprove of him working on a holy day, if he went to the diggings to look for fossils.

So Bill took Dad's old work jacket from the peg, and put that jacket on over his own one. He wound the long sleeves up to leave his hands free, put his cap on his head, and, quickly opening and closing the door, stepped out into the rain. The sky was still dark with heavy, roiling clouds that buffeted wind and rain at him.

Head down, Bill hurried through the village, the rain-loaded wind soaking him in moments, so that his clothes clung coldly to him. He hurried, squelching through the clay mud of the diggings field, which clagged heavily to his boots. Over by the washpit, Bill upturned a bucket by the pile of nodules waiting to be washed, and sat on it.

He reached for nodules, one after another, turning them and looking at them for signs of fossil life. His fingers turned red and raw with cold as he worked, and freezing rain lashed one side of his face to numbness. The nodules were all just dark lumps, until at last he found one devil's claw, then another, but he'd only get a halfpenny for each of those.

Dong, dong!

The church bell was calling people for the early Sunday service. Would Ma be up yet, shuffling her swollen legs, making herself some tea? He should have stayed at home, and brought tea to her in bed, like Dad did. Oh, he'd got it wrong again, hadn't he? Ma wasn't well enough for church. Besides, Mrs Buckle had called on Ma to complain about Bill bringing fossils to her door, and so now Ma was too embarrassed to show herself in church.

Bill threw a big nodule hard onto the pile. He was so stiff with cold and damp that he ached and it was an effort to move his fingers through the stones. To think that this place was once a part of hot Africa! And at another time was sea, with those devils' claws and snake-stone creatures swimming around in it.

Clack, clonk. Bill threw nodule after nodule back onto the pile.

Might Grantchester change again? he wondered. Would people look back and be surprised that it was ever a cold and wet and muddy place with houses and pubs and a school and a church? Would they look at the trench stripes over the land, and wonder what had made them, and why? Maybe it wouldn't even be people who looked and wondered such things. Dinosaurs went and people came, so maybe people would go too, and some other creatures replace us, thought Bill. But what sort? Dad said machines were taking over the world. Just look at how trains were replacing horses.

Hours passed, and Bill had only added one thunderbolt to the devil's toenails. His hands no longer felt anything as they picked up the nodules. *One last one,* he thought. He closed his eyes for a moment, sort of praying. *Make this a lucky one!* Then he'd go back home to warmth and food, and try to make Ma happy. Bill closed his eyes, dug deep into the pile as if it was a bran tub, and pulled out a nodule that was pleasingly big and lumpy. He tugged, but it wouldn't come. He opened his eyes. The nodule was awkwardly wedged between other stones, because it had lumpy wings sticking out from it.

'A vertebra!' Mr Seeley had shown Bill some of those in the museum. This one was as big as Bill's fist, so it must be from some big creature's spine. Two and sixpence worth, if he was lucky! Bill stood up . . . and the thing crumbled in his hands. It was just an odd-shaped clod of clay, not a fossil at all.

'You stupid –' He'd got it wrong again, failing Ma, failing the baby, failing Dad. All these hours for nothing! The rain suddenly turned into hard hail, throwing itself so viciously at Bill he closed eyes hot with tears, and staggered backwards . . .

. . . stepping onto nothing.

Chapter Fourteen

Bill fell, gasping with shock, and hitting his head and shoulders on the hard, wet earth walls as he fell before landing – *oomph!* – into freezing cold mud.

He lay for some moments, head dizzy, body hurting with cold and bruising, trying to work out where he was. He turned his head, and cold, gritty water washed over his face. He spluttered and coughed, pushing himself upright. And then he knew. He was at the bottom of a long, narrow, steep-sided trench.

Bill forced himself to sit, and then to stand, leaning against the mud. He reached his hands up towards the light of open air above him, but his fingertips were a good three or more feet below the top of the trench. There were steps at the end of every trench, so Bill waded, desperate to escape, but the earth steps had already washed away, turned to a brown waterfall of rain run-off.

'Oh no!' Bill lifted a foot and tried to climb the slight lumps that had been steps, but the slippery wet clay crumbled under him as soon as he put his weight on it. 'Oh, please!' Bill was sobbing now, pressing his hands into the mud walls, but the trench was too wide to let him press his hands and feet on either side, to work his way up.

He was trapped. The trench was an oversized grave, waiting to bury him with the ancient remains of other creatures from all those years ago. But he had a life to live *now!* A ma who needed him, and a baby sibling who depended on him, too. And Dad, away but trusting Bill to care for those others!

It was oddly quiet, deep in the trench. The sound of the storm's wind was muted now, and the hail didn't hit him sideways any more. But water was pouring off the field into the trench. Maybe if he waited long enough he could float up and out of it? But he'd freeze to death before that could happen.

And there was another problem. Water was already filling the layer of gravelly greensand that held the nodules below the slippery clay. That layer had been under-dug, hacked out below the main trench side in order to reach as many nodules as possible. That great weight of wet clay wall was unsupported. *It'll collapse,* realized Bill.

He gently pulled himself away from the side he'd been leaning on. *I've just got to get out!*

Bill's boots were under water, that was so cold it hurt his legs and numbed his feet. When he lifted one foot out, the other sank deeper. A part of the wall crumbled and fell into the water at his feet with a splash. 'Please, no!' Another splash, and suddenly Bill was frantic, clawing and kicking at the cold, hard, wet earth and stones of the trench wall, trying to work hand holds and foot holds to climb. But the soil either crumbled in his hands or it wouldn't give at all. Then mud began to fall from high above him, falling on his head, knocking him sideways and down, burying him. He scrambled backwards, away from the collapsing part, but he knew the rest of the earth would soon follow. 'Oh, please! Help me!' he shouted, as more trench mud slumped casually onto him, splashing into the bottom of the pit. 'Help!'

But who could hear Bill, down as deep as the bodies in the graveyard? Bill sat in the rising cold water now, trying to make his lungs work as he panicked at the thought of never being able to breathe again. All he could think was that he would be buried, and the world would go on, just as it always had done. Would he turn into a fossil, solidifying into stone over thousands – millions – of years? His legs might as well be stone already. He couldn't feel them. Tears, hot as new-made tea, scorched down his face. *Why do humans cry?* he wondered. He'd never seen an animal cry. *Did dinosaurs cry? Did the dinosaurs know they were dying out forever?*

Bill's heart ached with a yearning to know his baby brother or sister. He ached to put things right with Ma and Dad. He ached with a longing to have more life in which to find out more about . . . oh, everything. He wanted to live!

With a roar of fury, Bill stood and kicked his already dead-seeming legs, determined to try again to get out. He kicked away a patch of the greensand that slumped into the dirty water.

And that's when he saw the crocodile.

Chapter Fifteen

There, in the mud, was a big stone grin that was longer than Bill's arm. Embedded in the earth, but clearly visible, were two long rows of teeth, top and bottom. Was it a fossilized crocodile? From when Grantchester was in Africa? Mr Seeley would know. Bill crouched down to look, too interested in what he was seeing to be as panicked about the danger he was in as he had been moments before. There was a slight curve upwards in the long row of teeth, and a circle of stone above one end that was once clearly an eye. It seemed to Bill that the creature was smiling.

'Hello,' said Bill a bit stupidly. Was he so cold and numb that his mind had gone as daft as Mrs Coddle's? Was he imagining the animal, seeing it in the stones in that way you can sometimes imagine seeing faces in clouds?

Bill reached out a clumsy, red-raw finger, and touched the circle of eyehole above the teeth, wiping away mud to make it clearer. Then he wiped the whole long jaw with the soggy cuff of Dad's jacket, revealing more teeth. Bill's heart was thumping fast. He felt faint with cold and excitement and despair. He wanted to escape for himself, but now he also wanted to escape so that he could tell Dad and Mr Seeley about this crocodile! But the earth above the crocodile was crumbling and falling. *Aren't angels supposed to come to lift you away to Heaven when you die?* thought Bill. *Is this Hell, and my punishment for being wicked?* He lifted his head and roared at the sky. 'Oh, please!' he shouted. 'I'm sorry!'

And the line of sky suddenly had a blob of head in it, looking down at Bill. An angel?

'Sorry about what?' said the angel.

'Alf?' said Bill.

'What the bloomin' heck are you doing down there?' said Alf.

Bill couldn't answer. He just slumped, stunned, in the muddy water at the bottom of the trench, with one hand on the crocodile jaw.

'Are you stuck?' said Alf. Then the earth under his front foot gave way, splashing to land near Bill. 'Oi, don't you do that!' Alfie shouted at the earth, with fear in his voice, and he stepped back, out of Bill's view. Moments later, a plank slapped down to bridge over the trench, and then Alf was on it, crawling across it on hands and knees. 'Don't move, Billy boy,' he said. 'Wait here. I'm going over to get Dolly. And a rope.'

Bill's brain was almost as numb as his body. He wanted to close his eyes, but the wide-eyed crocodile grin challenged him not to.

'Here!' shouted Alf at last.

Slap! A rope hit the water beside Bill. Bill looked at it, but didn't move.

'Catch hold of it!' Alf was on the plank again. 'Oi, Billy boy, wake up!' A clod of earth hit Bill on the head, waking him from the cold that was paralysing his mind and body. Bill slowly reached for the rope. 'I've made a loop in it,' said Alf. 'Put it over your head and under your arms. I'll get Dolly to drag you up. I've tied the other end to her harness. Go on, Billy, get that rope over your head. Now!'

Slowly, painfully, Bill managed to hook the rope loop over his numb hands, using fingers that wouldn't work to grasp it. He heaved his right arm through. The left arm was too heavy with cold and pain to move at all.

'I don't think . . .'

'Yes, 'course you can!' said Alfie. 'Just do it, Billy! Then you can get to a warm fire. You can get home and eat food. Hurry up, because this trench is going to go any moment now.' Then, in a quieter voice, Alf said, 'Come on, Billy. Please! If you die, I'll kill you!'

Bill heard a wobble of caring in Alf's voice, and the surprise of that gave him the energy he needed. He took a deep breath, and, in spite of pain shrieking through his bones and muscles, he made that left arm go through the loop.

'Good,' said Alf, backing off the plank. 'Now keep your arms down.' His voice was going further away. 'Dolly, get moving.' He clicked his tongue. The tug on the rope around Bill made him cry out. But suddenly he was rising up out of the water, scraping against the trench walls.

'The croc–!' he began to say, but then bit his lip; he needed all of his energy to cope with the rough ride up the trench side. He twisted clumsily, trying to make his jacketed back take the worst of the drag against the stony side of the trench. Then he was out from the underground, up into wonderful big air and space and light, and Dolly and Alf in front of him at the end of the rope, and a sky with patches of blue among smudges of clouds above him. And the rain had stopped. Bill laughed and lay on his back. Then he said, 'There's a crocodile down there.'

'What are you on about now? You've gone daft, you have!' said Alf as he pulled the rope off over Bill's head.

'I don't think my legs will move,' said Bill. But, leaning

heavily on Alf's wiry body, the two of them managed to stagger all the way across the field and then across the farmyard to Dolly's stable.

'Get those wet clothes off,' said Alf, bending down to untie Bill's sodden boots. 'You've welded these flipping boots to your feet!' When the boots did come off, Bill's feet were grey-blue. He still couldn't feel them at all. For a moment Bill and Alf just looked at them. Then Alf grabbed a handful of straw and started rubbing Bill's feet with it. 'You've got to get warm, Billy. When little Frank got stuck in a ditch full of snow last winter, his lips went all blue like yours are now. Dad rubbed him all over with dripping to get the blood going round his arms and legs again. The doctor said that had saved Frankie's life. I'm going to pile straw around you to warm you. Is your dad still away? Do you want me to fetch your mam?'

Bill shook his head. He couldn't cope with Ma just now. All he could cope with was trying to hold himself together as the pain in his feet grew and his body's shaking seemed to threaten to rattle him apart. That and what he'd seen in the trench.

'That cr-cr-crocodile,' shivered Bill.

'Pull Dolly's blanket round you. That's it,' said Alf, draping it across his shoulders.

'There re-really is a —'

'How can there be a flipping crocodile in that trench?'

said Alf. 'You've just been seeing things that aren't there, like my dad does after too much beer.'

As time passed, Alf went home, and came back with a tin mug of cooling tea and a hunk of bread.

'Get this into you, and you'll start to talk better sense,' said Alf. 'I didn't tell on you,' he added. 'You'll lose your job if they find you've been messing about in the diggings.'

'Thanks.' Bill's shivering had subsided into deep, aching exhaustion. He sipped the tea and nibbled the bread, and that warmed him enough so that he could tell Alf how there really had been African animals living here because Grantchester was part of Africa once. He told him how he'd seen other crocodile things in the museum with Mr Seeley, and how he thought the market man, or even Mr Seeley, might pay a lot of money for a great big grinning head of the creature.

'What sort of a lot?' said Alf. 'More than for those ordinary fossils?'

'Much more, I should think,' said Bill. And it suddenly came to him how such money might make things better at home. It might mean that Dad didn't have to work away. It would buy food and coal for Ma and the baby. Bill sat himself more upright against the stable wall. 'D'you reckon we could ever get the croc out of that trench, though? Without Mr Gander knowing?'

'That trench was falling in,' said Alf. 'Your croc might be buried by now.'

'But that might be good thing,' said Bill. 'That way, the diggers won't see it and take it. We need it to sell, Alf, and they don't.'

'We?' said Alf.

Bill nodded. 'Of course "we", Alf. You got me out. Saved my life, I reckon. That crocodile's yours as much as mine.'

His legs and feet ached, but he could hobble home. Bill knew that Ma would be worrying about where he was. 'Anyway,' he said to Alf, 'what were you doing out at the diggings in the storm? Were you after fossils to sell, too?'

'No.' Alfie shrugged. 'I just had a feeling.'

'A feeling about what?' said Bill.

'You, I suppose,' said Alfie. Then he grinned. 'Or maybe it was the crocodile that called to me. "Alfie, Alfie, come and rescue Bill!" Tell you what, I'm going to put a marker by the trench where you came out, and make sure there's no croc showing. We'll have to think how to get it out without being seen. I want that money so I can get boots that fit and have a shine on them!'

'I want the money too,' said Bill. 'Thanks, Alf. And you too, Dolly,' he said, patting the huge horse on his way out her stable. 'See you both tomorrow.'

* * *

Bill felt light and happy, even though he was still numb
with cold. He'd survived. And he'd found something that
would excite Mr Seeley, and which just might make life
easier at home.

'Glory be, look at the state of you!' said Ma when Bill
opened the door. 'Don't take another step, Billy Ellwood,
until you've taken everything off. Is that your father's
jacket – or what's left of it? Come and get warm. I've
made some soup.'

Bill was happy to be told what to do, happy to be told
off, and even happier to be fed a bowl of hot soup. He
didn't mind anything at all. He was alive. And that strange
stone crocodile just might be a way to make everything
good again. As Ma talked on, Bill's mind floated away
from what she was saying, and instead tried to work out
how they might retrieve the crocodile fossil without the
company men noticing and taking it for themselves or
the owners.

Chapter Sixteen

The church bell tolled six o'clock, and Bill fumbled out of bed, stiff, his hands still red and sore from the day before. But he was determined to get to work before anybody else so that he could check on the state of the trench.

Downstairs, Bill poked and fed the fire to life in the grate, then hurried outside to see to the chickens. Back inside, he set the kettle over the fire, then called up to Ma. 'Kettle's on, Ma, and I'm off!'

'But . . .' called Ma. 'Billy!'

'I'll be back before dark,' said Bill. *With a surprise for you, if we get this right*, he thought. *Just you wait, Ma. The croc is going to mean that you can have white bread for breakfast and all the milk and candles you want, fine new cloth to make into gowns as smart as Mrs Buckle's, and, best of all, Dad home again. The baby, too, can have all it needs to grow strong. Then you'll see I'm not so bad after all. The baby will only ever know me as good.*

It was a cold day, but sunny now, and the sky was blue.

'Calm after the storm,' Mr Gander said, when he saw Bill arriving on the coprolite field.

Bother, thought Bill. *Now how am I going to get a look at the crocodile trench without him noticing?*

'Good lad for getting here early,' said Mr Gander. 'Get Dolly harnessed up straight away, will you? It's going to be a long day, what with all this mud.'

So Bill had no option but to begin the day by working with Dolly in the usual way, trying not to look too obviously over to the trench at the bottom of which was that croccy grin. He thought of Alf heading for school. When could he talk to Alf again? Bill's fingers were trembling clumsily as they worked the halter over Dolly's head, memories of the day before flooding back as he stood in the stable and the pool of straw that Alf had piled around him. Dolly's side felt wonderfully solid and warm and sure. Bill closed his eyes and just leaned against her for a moment to calm himself before leading her out and into the field.

'I'll buy you sticky buns when we've got the money for Croccy,' he told her. 'You and Alf both.'

As Bill buckled Dolly into the traces attached to the washer arm, the diggers gathered for their instructions from Mr Gander. Bill strained to hear Mr Gander telling them, 'You've all seen the storm damage to the trenches, so there's more danger than usual of collapse. I want four men on watch on each of the two trenches being dug. You diggers, you'll have to bucket out the water first thing.' Bill stopped harnessing Dolly and stood by her head, watching as Mr Gander pointed. 'I can't let any back into trench three as it is. Somebody's been messing about. It's got bad collapse that's more than just storm damage, I reckon. You don't know anything about it, do any of you?'

Uncle Fred and the others shook their heads.

'The surveyor's coming this morning, and he and I will look at it together. Meanwhile, you men can peg out a new trench.'

Bill breathed again. So the crocodile was safe, at least until this afternoon. Even then, the surveyor would only look down into the trench from above, wouldn't he? He wouldn't see the crocodile hiding under the main wall. But, as Bill got back to work, he couldn't help worrying that the crocodile would somehow snap his teeth and flash his grin at Mr Gander and the surveyor. And what if they did go down into the trench? Bill imagined that big croccy eye hole giving a wicked wink, teasing. He longed to talk to Alf about what they should do.

* * *

At morning break, Alf appeared at the washpit.

'Oi, young Smith, haven't I warned you before about coming on site?' said Mr Gander, as Alf come up to where Bill and Dolly were.

'Message for my dad,' said Alfie.

'And since when has your dad been eleven years old?' said Mr Gander. But he let Alf be, with an I've-got-my-eye-on-you warning look, as Alf went over to Bill.

'The surveyor's coming to look at that trench this afternoon,' whispered Bill. 'What if he finds the croc?'

'Is there really a crocodile there?' said Alf. 'I didn't know if you was talking sense or not yesterday.'

'It's as real as Dolly here,' said Bill.

'Right then,' said Alf. 'Let's dig it out tonight. Meet me once you can get away.'

'But what if the surveyor sees it this afternoon?' repeated Bill.

'Don't you worry!' said Alf, and he skipped over to talk to his dad.

'Alf, what are you . . . ?' began Bill, but Alf just grinned over his shoulder. After talking to his dad, Alf ran off back to school without another word, leaving Bill wondering what he'd done.

That afternoon, Uncle Fred volunteered to inspect the trench with the surveyor – 'Since I know the workings of that one inside out, sir.' For a moment, when Bill heard that, he panicked, then realized that this must be Alf's doing. It would be all right! Bill watched, leading Dolly slowly around the side of the washmill that gave him a view of trench three, and fast around the side that hid the trench from him. The stick that Alf had put as a marker was still in place. Bill saw that Uncle Fred busied the surveyor with something at the other end. He didn't even pause by the stick as they walked along the trench. Bill smiled, then felt a prickle of unease. He turned to notice that Mr O'Brien was watching him, watching and scowling and knowing that something was afoot.

Chapter Seventeen

Bill worried that evening about what to tell Ma about why he needed to go out so late. He didn't want to lie to her. 'I left something at the digging field,' wouldn't be a lie, but surely she'd want to know what that 'something' was, and 'a crocodile' as the answer would make for a complicated conversation and certain grounding. Then Ma herself gave Bill the excuse he needed.

'Get yourself an early night, Billy. You're all fidgety and peaky. You make me feel unsettled.'

She can't bear to have me near her, thought Bill. *Well, she won't know or care if I'm out.* Bill took a lit candle and made his way upstairs, snatching his jacket, and pocketing the firesteel and flint from the mantelpiece as he went. Quietly, he snuffed the candle out, and climbed out of Ma and Dad's bedroom window. Ma, big-bellied with the baby in her, and angry at Bill, wasn't likely to climb that ladder to see if he was in bed in the roof.

Bill scurried round to the back of the cottage, opened the shed, and took Dad's trowel, some sacking, and some of Dad's store of old candle stubs. He ran down to Bugs Row. There was still flickering candlelight downstairs at the Smiths', so Bill prowled around the village on his own for a bit, watching windows go dark, and the pubs empty of noisy men who made their way back to their homes or lodgings. The night stilled. A fox walked down the middle of the road, looked at Bill, then carried on its way. Then Alf made Bill jump, by appearing from round the corner, quiet as a cat, when Bill had been expecting him to come from his front door.

'Snuck out the back, didn't I?' said Alf. 'Mam and Dad are still up, and arguing. He's gone and lost his job. Gander's told him not to come back, and Ma's in tears.'

'Why?' Bill had an instant, horrible suspicion that it must be somehow his fault. 'What's happened?'

'He got into a fight with Mr O'Brien after work. Knocked one of O'Brien's teeth out. So now Gander's kept O'Brien and sacked me dad, even though Dad says the fight was started by O'Brien, so it's not fair. Flippin' Mr Gander!'

Bill knew about sackings that didn't feel fair. 'That's like my dad losing his job when it wasn't his fault either.

We'd best make sure to get the crocodile, sell it for lots of money, then both our dads can be laughing again.'

The still, cold, moonlit night was beginning to harden the ground with frost, so the muddy digging field was firmer underfoot than it had been during the day. Bill hoped that would mean that the mud walls of the trench were more stable. He took a length of rope from beside the washpit.

'Do you want to go down first?' he asked, as they got to the stick by the trench.

'No, you go down,' said Alf. 'You've seen the croc before, so you'll be better at finding it.'

Bill was glad of that. The crocodile felt 'his', even though he was sharing it with Alf. So Bill tied the rope around his middle, and Alf held one end of it. Facing backwards, Bill lowered himself down the mudslide that was all that was left of the steps there had once been at the head of the trench. Alf, feet braced, let out the rope to keep Bill's descent steady. Once at the bottom, Bill untied himself and carefully stepped along the dark trench, feeling his way with his hands along the mud.

'Can you see old Croccy?' said Alf after a while.

'Not yet,' said Bill. 'Pass me Dad's trowel, will you? I think I need to dig a bit to get at it.'

The moonlight came and went, as clouds covered or revealed its silvery sphere. But there was thick darkness eight foot down in the trench. Bill took the firesteel from his pocket and struck a spark to light a stub of candle. Alf threw the trowel down.

'Hurry up, won't you? It's blooming cold!' said Alf, blowing on his hands and slapping his arms.

Bill crouched down. Breathing hard and trying to keep his hands steady, he dug with Dad's trowel, digging out where the undercut layer had been filled in with fallen soil. All he could see was a mess of chalk and clay mud and stones. Then . . .

'There you are!' whispered Bill, touching the crocodile teeth, which were grinning at him dirtily. He called up to Alf. 'He's here! I knew it!' He carefully scraped the earth away to show the whole jaw and eye hole. 'D'you want to come down to see?'

Alf tied the rope end to a plank over the trench, and soon both boys were crouching low in the trench, looking at the crocodile. The flickering candlelight made the grinning jaw full of teeth and the wide-awake eye socket seem alive.

'It's some sort of dragon, instead of a crocodile, isn't it?' said Alf. 'The sort of dragon they had when Saint George was alive. Come on, let's get him out! D'you think the vicar would buy it, if we said it was Saint George's actual dragon?'

'I don't think Mrs Buckle would be pleased if he did!'

laughed Bill. 'But somebody will want it enough to pay well.' He felt a bit of a traitor, talking about selling the crocodile who'd waited to be found for all those thousands, maybe millions, of years. 'Careful,' said Bill as Alf attacked the earth around the crocodile head with a pointed stick he'd brought down with him. 'Be gentle.'

It took the light of five candle stubs, one after another, and hours of careful picking away at the soil around the jaw before it began to stand free of the trench wall, and all the time they were aware that the earth above where they'd dug might give way. The fossil could be buried again, and so could they, and nobody would know to come and rescue them. Bill's heart was thumping fast as they carefully picked and picked away. The clouds cleared and the moon shone like a ghostly sun, as they worked on and on, over and under and around the fossil head.

'How are we going to get it out of the trench?' said Alf.

'We'll have to hoist it,' said Bill. 'It'll be heavy. And then we've got to hide it, but not in Manor Farm shed with the other fossils. This one's worth too much to let everyone see it. I don't trust Mr O'Brien, especially after what he did to your dad.'

Alf hawked and spat to show what he thought of Mr O'Brien.

The crocodile head was very heavy and awkward to manoeuvre, but it finally came away from the earth that had held it since before Bible times.

'Is there more of the animal in there, do you think?' said Alf, holding the candle stub to where the crocodile head might have joined a body.

'Must be,' said Bill. 'We could look . . .'

'No time left tonight,' said Alf. 'We've got to get this head somewhere safe. We can look for the body another night. Then we'd find out properly if it is a crocodile or a dragon or something else.'

They heaved the head up onto the surface, and then climbed out of the trench.

'Let's take a barrow to wheel it over to yours,' said Alf. 'We can hide it in your chicken run. Or –'

'Shh!' Bill clapped a hand over Alf's mouth, and pulled him down to the ground. 'Ow!' Alf had bitten him. 'Shh!' hissed Bill again. 'Look! There's somebody there!'

They rolled onto their fronts, and looked to the far side of the field by Manor Farm where a tall figure with a lantern stood in silhouette against the moonlit sky. The lantern beamed a wedge of light that bounced as the man walked.

'Oh, no!' Alf groaned. 'It's me dad! He's poaching! Watch. He's going to get a hare, I bet.'

Fred tipped his lantern to light a patch of ground, then he stopped, statue still.

'What's he –?' began Bill.

'Just watch,' said Alf. 'You'll see how he gets them.'

Bill felt the cold of the frosty earth seeping into him. He longed to move, to get the crocodile head hidden and himself to his warm bed. Alf nudged Bill, and pointed. Bill could just make out a tall-eared shape of a hare, frozen still in the light of Fred's lantern. Fred lifted a thick stick. Bill closed his eyes, not wanting to see the stick come down to kill the hare.

Alf snorted quiet laughter. 'You'd eat the pie soon enough,' he said.

That was true, thought Bill.

Fred had picked up the limp hare, and was moving off now, towards the church and Manor Farm. The boys scrambled to their feet. It took all their strength, heaving an end each, to get the long crocodile's grinning stone head into a works wheelbarrow.

'You pull the barrow from the front while I push,' said Bill. They heaved the barrow, with its lopsided load, over the field. 'The back of your house is nearer than mine,' said Bill. 'Is there anywhere we could hide it there?'

But Alf didn't answer. He was looking towards the farm. 'That can't be the sun coming up already, can it?' said Alf.

Bill looked. 'That's not the sun!' he said. 'That's a fire! The farm's on fire!'

They could hear shouts, calling for help, from the

direction of the fire.

'That's Dad shouting!' said Alf. 'Quick! Dump the head. We've got to go and help!'

Chapter Eighteen

They struggled with the heavy wheelbarrow, over the frosted mud to the bit of falling down wall at the end of the Smith back yard.

'Dump the head here,' said Alf. 'We can put it somewhere better later.' Alf upended the barrow, and Bill cradled the stone head as it slid to the ground. 'Nobody'll see it behind there,' said Alf. 'Come on, Dad needs us!' Bill pulled grass and weeds over the sack-wrapped head. 'Come on!' said Alf again, and both boys ran with the barrow back over the field, dumping it before they ran into the farmyard.

There was shouting coming from where the fire lit up Manor Farm.

'It's the diggers' shed that's burning,' panted Bill. He thought of the stone snakes and devil's claws and thunderbolts that he had stored there, and then he thought of something he minded about much more than any of them. 'Dolly!' Her stable was next door to the shed.

The long shed was ablaze, the fire roaring flames and smoke into the night-time sky as if it was a dragon. Mr Lilley was there in his nightgown, shouting orders at a couple of servant men who lived in the manor, and at his sons. More people were coming, running from the village. Bill saw Mrs Lilley, looking shockingly different from her daytime appearance, in a nightgown, her hair in a long plait down her back. She was working the pump to fill the buckets and pans and barrows being brought by the men.

'Dad!' shouted Alf.

Uncle Fred was one of the men swinging buckets of water at the fire. Alf grabbed a bucket to join them, passing buckets, hand to hand. Bill ran straight to the stable next to the shed. The fire hadn't jumped the gap to set it alight yet. Thank goodness it was a windless night, thought Bill.

'Dolly? Where are you, Dolly girl?' he called, peering into the darkness. She usually had her big head looking over the stable door, but now she was cowering in the back of her stall. Bill pulled the bolt, and stepped into the hot darkness. Dolly was pressing against the back wall. Bill could feel her fear tensing the smoky air as he reached out to touch her. 'There, girl. There we are, Doll. I'm going to get you out now. Don't you worry. You'll soon be safe and s—'

Crash! The sound of collapsing timbers and shattering tiles was followed by choking-thick smoke billowing into the stable, through the doorway. Dolly's loud, terrified neighing shook the air, and she reared up, huge and heavy, in the small stable. Bill had to dodge fast to avoid her iron-shod hooves as they came crashing down.

'There, girl,' he said, feeling with one hand for the halter he knew he'd find on the wall hook, and laying the other hand, steadying, on Dolly's flank. There was more shouting from outside.

'Get back!'

'Stand away!'

'Shed's going!'

Bill's heart was pounding. He could hardly breathe in the smoke. He was coughing, sweat pouring off him and making his hands slip as he reached up to loop the halter over Dolly's big head.

'You're all right, my lovely. There, there, girl.' In spite of the smoke inside the stable, big, strong Dolly was resisting moving towards the flare and roar of fire beyond the open door. *I'm not strong enough to force her out,* thought Bill, *but the fire's spreading!* He pulled off his jacket and held it over Dolly's head so that she couldn't see the flames, and he felt her relax enough for him to lead her, clattering and skittering over the cobbled yard, into fresh air . . . just as the shed slumped within a shower of sparks and a billowing of black smoke.

'Well done, there. That's Bill Elwood, is it?' said Mr Lilley, slapping Bill on the back, and then stroking a hand down Dolly's neck. 'Take Dolly to the small field, and make sure there's water for her.' Then he turned back to the yard where the men were sousing and beating out flames in the collapsed mass of beams and tiles that had been the diggers' shed.

Bill was exhausted. He ached all over. His mind seemed to float somewhere outside his body. He leaned against Dolly's massive shoulder as she clopped across to the small field. The sun really was coming up now, pinking the rim between earth and sky towards Trumpington, giving a pale light, so that lanterns were no longer needed. Bill opened the gate to the field, and led Dolly in. Head down, she pulled at the grass, almost as if it was a normal day.

'I'll see you later, girl,' he told her, stroking her neck. Then Bill went slowly back to the yard to make sure that Alf and Uncle Fred hadn't been hurt when the shed had collapsed. They were working together, still throwing buckets of water onto the smouldering remains of shed to damp down the last of the flames. Bill suddenly missed his own dad badly.

'Get yourself home, lad,' said Mr Nutter. 'You look all in.'

So that's what Bill did.

It was strange, walking through the village as day was breaking and yet Bill hadn't even gone to bed yet, let alone slept. People who had slept were emerging from their homes, wanting to know what was going on up at Manor Farm, but Bill's head was down. He didn't answer. His mind was filled with the fire and Dolly and that crocodile head, and he was too exhausted to share any of it just yet. Especially since the person he really wanted to share it with was Dad.

Ma, fully dressed, snatched open the door when she saw Bill coming up the road, and she pulled him inside.

'Oh, Billy, what have you gone and done now?' she said, one hand to her forehead, the other resting on her swollen tummy.

'I haven't . . .' began Bill, but he didn't know what it was that he should say that he hadn't done.

'I know that you were out last night, Billy!' fussed Ma, a hand to her pale cheek. 'I went up and I found your bed empty and your clothes gone, and I thought, "He's gone off poaching with Alf and Fred Smith, after all that I've told him not to." Is that where you were, Billy? Stealing? You could get caught and sent to gaol! Or worse!' For all she was frail, Ma had firm hold of Bill's shoulders now, and she was shaking him. 'You'll drive me to an early grave, Billy Ellwood, you really will! Where I've gone wrong, I just don't know. Blood will out, is all I can think! Oh, Billy!'

'Stop it, Ma!' said Bill, shrugging her hands from his shoulders. He leaned against the wall, hardly able to stand, he was so exhausted. 'I wasn't poaching!'

'Then what were you doing?'

Bill closed his eyes for a moment, then opened them and said, 'I was digging out a big fossil. With Alf.'

Ma's eyebrows went up. 'In the middle of the night? So you *were* with a Smith! And where is this big fossil, then?'

'It's, well, it's somewhere. But there's been a fire and I've been helping. Oh . . .' Bill shook his head. He just didn't have the energy to tell it all, to explain. He didn't think Ma would believe him even if he did tell the full truth of it all.

Tears were pouring down Ma's cheeks now. 'Mrs Buckle says that fossils are the work of the devil. I don't want you having anything more to do with fossils or those Smiths! Ever since they came to the village, you've changed, Billy. You're dragging your father and me down.' She slumped into her chair and turned her face away from him.

Chapter Nineteen

Bill, filthy with soot and mud and sweat and tears, lay on top of his bed and slept the whole of the next day through. He awoke, cold and thirsty and hungry, and not sure what time or even which day of the week it was. Then a rush of memories of the previous night came back to him. Croccy the fossil. The fire! Ma not believing him when he'd told the truth. Ma saying that he was dragging her and Dad down. Ma saying he was to have nothing more to do with fossils or Alf. And now, on top of all that, he must have missed a day's work. He'd be out of a job, just like Dad and Uncle Fred!

Bill curled himself up small. The only person who perhaps had the power to put things right was Mr Seeley. Would Mr Seeley buy the crocodile for his museum? Stiff and dirty and cold, Bill crept down his ladder into his parents' room, and then down the stairs. He could hear Ma talking with Mrs Coddle again. Ma looked up as Bill came into the room. Her face was grey and drawn. Her hands were holding each other tightly.

'Tea, Billy?' she said stiffly. The tea was cold and bitter, but it was liquid and refreshing.

'You look like a chimney sweep boy, Billy!' said Mrs Coddle. 'I was just telling your mother, Billy, they've taken Fred Smith away.'

Bill stopped drinking. 'Taken him away to where? Why?'

'To gaol, that's where! For that fire,' said Mrs Coddle. 'They say Fred Smith was first there at the fire, and with a lantern and all, so it's clear for all to see that it was him that done it. Him having a grudge against the mining company, what with Mr Gander having sacked him, and all. It's a bad do, though. Think of poor Lil Smith, with all those children!'

Bill smashed his cup down on the table. 'Don't say such rubbish lies, you silly old woman! Uncle Fred was poaching last night, that's all! He wouldn't –'

'So,' said Ma, quietly quivering with emotion. 'If you know that Fred Smith was poaching, Billy, you *must* have been wi–'

'No, Ma!' Bill leaned over his mother, almost spitting in her face with fury. 'We just saw him. I told you what

Alf and I were doing. But you won't believe me, so what's the point of me telling you anything?'

'Well, it's all around the village,' said Mrs Coddle, tutting her tongue against what teeth she still had. 'Who'd have thought it, eh? They've taken him off to the cells. Poor Lil . . .'

Bill got up and headed for the door.

'And where do you think you're going now?' said Ma.

'I'm going to see the Smiths.'

'No!' Ma reached out a hand to grab him back.

'The Smiths are my friends,' said Bill. 'You should stick by friends when they are in trouble.' He slammed out of the door and along the road. He was still filthy, but he didn't care about that. What he cared about was Alf and Uncle Fred.

They couldn't be right about Uncle Fred, could they? he wondered momentarily, but knew in his gut that they were wrong. Yes, Fred was breaking the law when he took that hare, but it was to be cooked and eaten by his family. How could that be so bad? A father was supposed to provide for his family, wasn't he? Bill wondered if his own dad would have got to the point of poaching, if that gardening job hadn't come up. He wouldn't have blamed him if he had. But he also knew that the Smiths did have money for food, at least until Fred lost his job. And he knew that Fred enjoyed poaching for the sport of it.

Gents killed creatures for sport when they had no need at all for the meat. Wasn't that worse than what Fred did? Bill didn't feel he even knew what was right or wrong any more. But, poacher or not, he didn't believe Fred Smith was an arsonist. Nor was he stupid. If he'd set the fire going, he'd have hidden away from it, surely?

Bill didn't knock on the Smiths' door in Bugs Row, but pushed straight in to find Auntie Lil, hair hanging loose, sitting on a stair with children around her as she sobbed into her apron. She looked up with hope as the door opened, but Bill saw that hope disappear from her eyes when she saw it was only him standing there, and not Fred.

'They've taken him,' she told Bill.

'I heard,' said Bill.

'They say he set that fire going! They say he'll get transported to the other side of the world! Either that, or . . .' She clamped a hand over her mouth.

'But he didn't do it,' said Bill.

'I keep telling her,' said Alf running in. 'Bill and me, Mam, we *saw* Dad, and he was poaching, that's all. I've told Mr Gander what's up.' Alf put an arm around his mother's shoulders. 'Don't worry, Mam, Bill'll tell Mr Lilley what Dad was doing. I tried, but he took no notice of me. Likely he'll listen proper to Bill, seeing that Bill's from a better sort of family.'

Ma would like Alf saying that, thought Bill.

Alf shoved Bill back out of the door. 'We've got to go to Manor Farm now, and tell them Lilleys. Come on.'

'But, Alf, your dad *was* lamping hares,' pointed out Bill. 'Do we tell them that? That's against the law, so if we say that we'll put him into other trouble.'

'Yeah, we do tell them!' said Alf. 'They'll believe that, won't they? It's what Dad does, and everyone knows it. It explains him being there. And it's the truth, the same as him not lighting that fire is the truth. All right, Dad'll have to pay a fine, or spend time in gaol, but, Bill, they're talking about hanging him dead!'

'Mr Lilley would never let them do that,' said Bill, running to keep up with Alf.

'It was Mr Lilley who told the law it was Dad who'd done it, because everyone's saying about Dad being there first, and with a lantern,' panted Alf. 'Mr Gander won't stand up for Dad either. Says he wasn't there at the time so he can't vouch for anybody.'

'Well, that's true,' said Bill. 'But we can vouch for your dad. You and me. We *were* there, and there wasn't time between him getting that hare and us seeing the fire, already big and glowing, for him to have lit it.'

They thumped on the front door of the big Manor farmhouse. Mr Lilley opened it. He was clean now, in a smart jacket, and clearly in the middle of his dinner, wiping a napkin over his mouth. Bill was suddenly conscious of still being grubby from the night's adventures. So was Alf.

'Boys,' said Mr Lilley. 'Yes, yes, I've sixpences for all the children who helped last night.' He reached into a pocket, and handed over two tiny silver coins.

'Thank you, Mr Lilley, sir, but it's not that,' said Bill, talking fast. 'I've come to tell you that I saw Mr Fred Smith out poaching last night, and then I saw the fire, and it was already well alight. He couldn't have got there and lit the fire that fast. Nobody could.'

'Is that so?' Mr Lilley was frowning.

'Alf and me, we saw Uncle Fred,' began Bill, but Mr Lilley interrupted.

'*Uncle* Fred?' Mr Lilley's eyebrows shot up. 'So Fred Smith is your uncle, is he, Bill? And he's your father, of course, Alf. So you would defend him.'

'But he's innocent!' said Bill.

'Please, Mr Lilley!' begged Alf.

Mr Lilley shook his head. 'There's nothing I could do, even if I was inclined to,' he said. 'Smith was taken to the county gaol on Castle Hill by the constabulary, and will stand trial in due course. It's all out of my hands.'

'But it isn't right!' said Alf. 'Dad was just poaching.'

'Ah yes!' laughed Mr Lilley. 'I can believe that! Fred Smith may not have been back in the village for long, but he's already well known for that particular hobby. Do you really think adding to the list of charges against him will help him?' said Mr Lilley. 'I'll do you a kindness, Alfred, and not mention that particular fact to the constabulary.'

'But it's the truth!'

'Besides, the magistrate won't take evidence from anyone so closely related to the accused. If you want to help Mr Smith, his only hope now is a really clever lawyer.' Mr Lilley was closing the door, preparing to go back to this meal, then he paused. 'But I really wouldn't waste your time and money on that. It seems clear enough to me that Smith had a grudge since losing his job. He now owes me a large sum of money for a new shed. I, for one, won't be sorry to see him gone from the village.' The door was almost closed when Mr Lilley had another thought and opened it again. 'And what exactly were you two boys doing out in the night, in any case? Learning how to poach? Or was it the two of you who set fire . . .'

'No!' said Bill. 'We were out digging . . .'

' . . . for a dragon,' said Alf.

'Oh, really!' said Mr Lilley, shaking his head, and now he did close the door, very firmly.

For a moment or two the boys just stood looking at that shut door.

'He didn't even . . .' began Alf, and swung his leg back as if he was going to kick the door.

'Don't!' said Bill, tugging him away. 'That'll only make

them think we're all badduns. We've got to find a way to help your dad, not make it all worse.'

'But how?' Alf had tears in his eyes. 'We couldn't ever afford a lawyer.'

'Yes we will,' said Bill.

'How?'

'With the crocodile dragon,' said Bill. 'We'll take that fossil head to Mr Seeley. He's nice. He's fair. He'll give us the money.'

But he didn't know how they'd get Croccy to Mr Seeley without being seen, nor how much Mr Seeley would pay or a lawyer would charge, nor how long they had before Uncle Fred's trial. But Bill couldn't see the point in saying all that to Alf. He looked him square in the eyes. 'The dragon will save your dad, you'll see.'

Chapter Twenty

The following week was a muddle of panic and hope.

A letter came from Dad. Ma read it while Bill was at work, but then she read bits of it out to him as they ate a watery stew that evening.

'*It's a grand place,* Dad says. *Not that I've seen inside beyond the servants' quarters, except for the odd peep through a big window to see pictures of a size you wouldn't believe, along with stuffed animals and birds. My room, shared with one of the under gardeners, is above the stables, so it's warm enough and we're fed well in the kitchens, but it isn't home. Poor man.'* Ma shot Bill a look. 'If only he hadn't lost his job here.'

'Does he say when he's coming home?' said Bill.

Ma turned the letter over. 'He says he'll be home on Christmas Eve. *For a few days.*' Ma gave Bill a sharp look.

'He says that he's sure you are taking good care of me.'
She shook her head. 'What would he think if he knew about the poaching and the fire?'

There'd been no coprolite digging the day after the fire. And now the company was closing the diggings for the Christmas break early so that a new shed could be built. There would be no more work or earnings for Bill until after Boxing Day, now. He worried about buying more coal to keep Ma and the baby warm. But at least there was now a good chance to fetch the fossil head from behind Bugs Row, unseen by Mr O'Brien or any of the others – who'd been put to work at Manor Farm, clearing the mess from the fire. School had closed for Christmas, so Alf was free too.

Bill called round at Alf's, wanting to plan how they'd get the crocodile head into Cambridge, and he found Auntie Lil and Lizzie were struggling with sheet-washing from one of the colleges in an effort to earn money for a lawyer. The Smiths' cramped home was even more than usually clammy, damp with sheets strung on ropes across the room, trying to dry as it rained coldly outside. Auntie Lil had been to see Fred in gaol. He was frightened, she said.

'I've seen Fred in a lot of states before,' she told Bill. 'But never scared, and that's what's terrifying me.'

'Bill and me, we'll go and see him, Mam,' said Alf.

'We'll cheer him up.'

'His trial's to be when the lawyers get back to work after Christmas, so in a couple of weeks' time,' said Auntie Lil.

'But Bill and me have got a plan, Mam,' said Alf. 'Don't you worry.'

Lil didn't ask what the plan was, but she gave them both a small smile as she heaved another sheet over a washing line.

When Bill got home to find Mrs Coddle with Ma, he told them what he'd heard from Auntie Lil.

'Uncle Fred said that the shed was already on fire when he got to it. He shouted to wake the Lilleys, then helped to put the fire out. He said the fire must have been started by somebody, there being no lightning or fire or candle nearby to have done it by accident, but he didn't know who it could be.'

'Well, he *would* say that, wouldn't he?' said Ma.

'That's it,' said Mrs Coddle. 'Why, I remember a man once . . .' and on she went, with a tale Bill didn't want to hear. It seemed that Ma didn't want to hear it either, as she cut in.

'Billy, one of Mr Gander's men called round when you were out. He said that your fossils that were in the shed had gone black in the fire, but were still there if you want them. But he said to fetch them quick because they'll throw them away if you don't. I said I'd tell you.'

'I can sell them, Ma,' said Bill.

Ma said nothing, and Mrs Coddle resumed her tale.

Bill collected Alf, and they went together to where the charred remains of the diggers' shed was now an acrid-smelling patch of land with the blackened brick foundations marking where walls had been. Clay tiles lay smashed. Burned and broken timbers lay in damp grey ash. To one side was a black jumble of odd-shaped things that had survived the heat of the fire. There was a shovel pan and a pitchfork prong with no handles. A dented lantern. A tin cup, which must have belonged to one of the diggers and been used for his lunch. A spring. A buckle. And there were some of Bill's and Alf's ammonites and devil's claws, which had been on the display plank in the shed.

'There are only five here,' said Bill. 'There were ten. The others must have got lost in all the mess.'

'Or O'Brien's stolen them,' said Alf, turning a devil's claw over in his hand. 'Do you think that market man might take them, all black like this? That dragon head needs cleaning too, doesn't it, if it's to fetch a good price?'

So, early next morning, they pumped and carried water to put in Lil Smith's tin bath in their yard. They climbed the wall, and carefully heaved Croccy's head up and over, and unwrapped the sacking. They used Alf's mam's scrubbing brush to clean away the grit and soil to reveal the teeth and the eye hole and the jaw more clearly. The water was cold and their sore hands stung.

'He's looking good,' said Bill. That fossil grin cheered him. 'Let's wrap him and hide him again before your lot come out and see it. We can hide him at mine, in the chicken run.' Bill wanted Croccy back on his territory. He was afraid that there were too many Smiths here who would be sharper to notice things than poorly Ma, who was more often than not stuck in the house.

Bill and Alf made a sort of sling from the sacking, and staggered down the street with Croccy to Bill's, leaving the smaller fossils soaking in the tin bath.

'We'll never carry it all the way into Cambridge,' panted Alf, swapping the load from one shoulder to another.

'Then Mr Seeley will have to ride out on his horse to see it,' said Bill. They left the head, covered, in a corner of the chicken run.

'Come on, let's find Mr Seeley now,' said Bill. 'It's market day, and we can go and visit your dad too.' Bill's own dad would be home the next day, he realized, and he suddenly felt happier.

It was sunny now but cold as they made their way over the meadows with the small fossils in their pockets. Alf also had a basket that his Ma had made him bring.

'What's in it?' asked Bill.

'Things for Dad,' said Alf. 'Christmas comforts, Mam said. There's a loaf of new bread. Some good new knitted mittens. Those are from your ma.'

'Are they?' said Bill.

'She sent that Mrs Coddle over with them. Mrs Coddle said your ma said the mittens was for Mam, but Mam said Dad's the one needing comfort, and they're big enough to stretch to a man's hands. And there's this scarf.' Alf pulled out a corner of something soft and brown. He grinned. 'I might as well warm it up for him, eh?' Alf wound the scarf around his neck, tucking the ends into the front of his jacket. 'It's lovely,' he said. 'Feel that.'

'Who is that from?' said Bill.

'Posh, isn't it?' said Alf, fingering the woven wool. 'It's from the vicar's wife, that Mrs Buckle. She came round asking after Dad. Christian duty, I suppose. Mam thinks the sun shines out of her backside, just because she gives us things.'

'My ma does too,' said Bill.

'I don't like her,' said Alf. 'Why does she have to cut all the bows and fancy bits off the dresses she hands down to our girls?'

'So that they don't look as grand as her own girls, I suppose,' said Bill. He went quiet, then he said, 'Would God prefer people with extra bows and whatnot on their clothes, or ones who dress plain, do you think?'

'What are you on about now?' said Alf.

'Well, think of Jesus on that cross in the church. He's wearing nothing except a clout of cloth around his bum. No frills or bows on it, and that was God's own son. Even in pictures of Jesus in everyday life, he's just in a sort of gown thing, isn't he? Bare feet. No hat. Not gentry, even for olden times, when you think of it.'

'So, going barefoot makes me more like Jesus than the vicar is?' said Alf. 'You're daft, you are, Billy boy, but you do make me laugh!'

They went to Sidney Sussex College first of all.

'Stop, Billy. They won't let us into a grand place like this!' said Alf, as Bill stepped through the stone archway towards the porters' lodge.

'It's where Mr Seeley lives,' said Bill. 'He said to come here to find him if I ever found an interesting fossil, so I am. Don't you worry, he's going to be really pleased about Croccy, and soon we'll have the money to help your dad get free again.'

'You go in, then,' said Alf. 'I don't want more trouble. I'm staying here.'

So Bill boldly opened the porters' lodge door and went in.

It wasn't long before Bill came out again. He was scowling.

'What?' said Alf.

'Mr Seeley's not blooming well there,' said Bill. 'He's gone home to his family for Christmas. That porter man wouldn't tell me where that is. He said he didn't know when he'd be back either.' He didn't say to Alf what was most worrying him, and that was whether or not Mr Seeley would be back in time to buy the big fossil before Uncle Fred's trial was due. But he saw Alf thinking it all the same. 'Come on, let's go to the market with the little fossils, and then to your dad.'

Cambridge market was festive with holly and mistletoe hanging from stall-roof poles. There were geese and turkeys and chickens and hams and sides of beef on show, making Bill feel hungry.

'Look at that!' said Alf, pointing to a caravan on wheels, beside Great St Mary's church. A woman in the doorway had bright cloth wound around her head, and her arms jangled with bangles.

'Have your fortunes read, young gentlemen,' she said. 'Just sixpence for me to tell you what your futures hold.'

'Do you think she really could tell what's going to happen to Dad?' said Alf.

'I don't see how she could know the future, since it's not yet happened,' said Bill. 'We'll do your dad more good by getting money for a lawyer to bend the future in the right direction and to get him safe home than asking for her guess at things.'

'Where's the fossils stall, then?' said Alf.

Bill pointed.

The fossil seller was busy with a woman in a hooped skirt, bonnet and shawl. She was fingering a number of ammonite swirls that had been cut and polished.

'It's to be a paperweight,' she told the man.

'Then the heavier the better,' said the market man.

'Does that mean the largest, and therefore the priciest?' asked the lady, eyebrows raised.

'Well, yes, Madam, but for you, and because it's the season of goodwill, it would be my honour to reduce the price,' smirked the market man. He glanced over to where Bill and Alf were nudging each other and laughing, and he jerked his head to tell them to push off. They didn't. When the woman had bought what she wanted, he turned to them.

'Not you again,' he said, looking at Bill. 'What are you after this time?'

'We've brought some fossils for you to buy,' said Bill, bringing the ammonites and devil's toenails from his pockets.

The man peered at them. 'Grubby things,' he sneered. Most of the soot had come off when they'd washed them, but not all, and it was true that the fossils were dull compared with his polished specimens.

'Cut them, and they'll be good as new inside, like the one that lady bought,' said Bill.

'Oh, so you're an expert now that you've talked to that Mr Seeley, are you?'

'I know that these are worth a couple of shillings,' said Bill.

'Couple of pennies, more like.' The man turned away.

'We've got a dragon head as well,' said Alf. 'Only it's heavy, so it would have to be fetched with a cart if you wanted it.'

'Shush, Alf!' said Bill. 'That's not for here!'

'Dragon?' scoffed the man. 'There's no such –'

'No, there isn't,' agreed Bill. 'But there are these fossils.'

'A fossil monster, then,' said Alf, not to be deterred. 'Billy here's seen one like it in that museum, haven't you, Billy?'

'Mmm,' agreed Bill. Might the market man give them a good enough price to pay for a lawyer? Bill doubted it, but beggars can't be choosers, he thought. That was something Mrs Coddle liked to say. So he told the man, 'It's a kind of crocodile head, like the one found by that lady fossil hunter, and it's got some Latin name that I can't remember.'

'Oh, yes? How big is it? What is there of it?' The man was interested now, in spite of another customer looking at his display.

Alf held out his arms. 'It's a whole jaw full of teeth about this long. And an eye hole. It's smiling, too, so that would make people more likely to buy it, wouldn't it? Who'd want a grumpy fossil when they can have a happy one? That's got to add to the price.'

'And where exactly is it?' said the man.

'We've hidden it in –' began Alf.

'It's locked up safe,' said Bill.

The market man was actually rubbing his hands together. He saw Bill notice, and did a little laugh. 'Cold today, isn't it?' he said. 'Tell you what, would you boys let me buy you a hot toddy at the Queen's Head?'

Alf opened his mouth, but Bill jumped in first. 'No, thank you, sir. We just want to sell these fossils today, and then we have to go somewhere.'

'Well,' the man's hands were winding round each other now, 'seeing that it's the day before Christmas Eve and all, I'll give the two of you a whole shilling for the grubby little ones.' He pushed their fossils from the table into a box behind his stall, then he took money from a tin. 'Fair shares, is it?' he said, 'Sixpence each, is it? Happy Christmas, lads!' And he handed a small silver sixpence to each of them. 'How about that?'

'Thank you, sir!' said Alf.

'And, I'll tell you what else,' said the man, 'I'll make an offer that's just as generous for that dragon head you mentioned. Um, let me see now. I'll offer you five whole shillings for that one. Five shillings . . . oh, and a goose for your family Christmas meal. How's about that?'

'That would be –' began Alf, beaming wide.

'Alf!' whispered Bill in warning, pulling him away from the stall.

'What?'

'Perhaps your pal doesn't want five shillings?' said the man to Alf, giving Bill a sharp look. 'I can't promise that deal will hold if you don't make up your mind now. As you've seen from those sixpences you have in your pockets, you've caught me in a generous mood today, but who's to say how long that mood will last?'

Bill just picked up the basket of things for Uncle Fred, and walked away.

Alf hurried after him. 'What's the matter with you?' said Alf, as Bill walked quickly towards Castle Hill. 'We could be drinking hot toddies now, and carrying home a great fat –'

'We're going to see your dad, aren't we? And Croccy's worth more than that,' said Bill. 'A heap more than what he said.'

'How do you know that, all of a sudden?'

'Otherwise why would he be so keen for us to give it to him for that amount?' said Bill.

'Oh, I know he was offering hot drinks and the goose

to make us willing to take a poor price,' said Alf. 'But, to tell the truth, Billy, I don't care what the thing's worth, so long as it pays enough to help my dad, and five shillings might do that. Your Mr Seeley might not get back in time before Dad's trial. It's all right for you with your fancy, rich family –'

'We owe rent money and we owe the doctor, until Dad comes home with his wages,' said Bill. 'But, yes, your dad is the most important one just now. All the money can be for him.' Bill handed his sixpence to Alf.

'Thanks, Bill. But we still need –'

'I know,' said Bill. They were walking past the fortune teller's caravan, and there was a queue of people outside it now, chatting and holding their sixpences ready to pay. 'Tell you what,' said Bill with a laugh. 'There is a way we might make more money out of Croccy than we can by selling it to that market man. And it would mean that we'd still have Croccy to sell, if Mr Seeley wants it!'

Alf stopped still and looked at Bill.

'How?'

'We could put the dragon on show,' said Bill.

Chapter Twenty-One

The boys discussed Bill's dragon show idea all the way up Castle Hill towards the county gaol. Would it only be the smiley head on show? Who would pay to see it? Where could the show be? How much would they charge? When would they do it?

'We've got to think how to make it look good,' said Bill. 'I've seen flowers on display on stands in a show, but nothing like our fossil.'

'I went to the fair in Ipswich,' said Alf. 'They had a lady there with a beard you could pay to see, and she was dressed all fancy with feathers in her hat as well as having her beard.'

They were so engrossed in talk that it came as a shock when they were suddenly standing at the entrance to the county gaol. There were fat stone pillars either side of the door, and a great arch with a portcullis over it. 'Go on, Alf, knock,' said Bill.

Inside, the gaol was dark and cold, with echoing shouts and clanking metallic sounds. Bill clenched his fists by his sides as he, and Alf carrying the basket, followed the gaoler towards the cells.

The stone cells themselves had high windows, criss-crossed with bars, and a wall of bars on the inside. The jailer stopped at a cell holding five men, all of them bearded and smelly, pale and hugging themselves for warmth and comfort. Those men looked frightened, thought Bill. It was a shock when he suddenly realized that one of them had Uncle Fred's foxy long nose.

'Alfie?' said Uncle Fred, coming to the cage bars.

Alf said nothing. Staring at his dad, he simply handed over the bread, the mittens and the scarf, one at a time.

'Well, that's just the ticket for keeping me warm!' said Fred, putting the scarf around his neck, then pulling the mittens onto his hands. Bill saw the other desperate-eyed convicts noting the food and the scarf and mittens. Convicts. Bill checked himself. Just because Fred was here didn't mean he was a convict. Why had he thought that word? You had to be convicted before you are a convict. Mr Lilley and half the village might have convicted Fred Smith, but no judge or jury had, not yet. Bill wanted to ask Uncle Fred about the night of the fire, but the gaoler was standing there, watching and listening. He didn't want the gaoler to hear about the poaching, if that would make the law think worse of Uncle Fred. Anyway, it should be Alf asking his dad questions, not Bill.

'And how's your family keeping, Bill?' said Uncle Fred, just as if they were sitting in a parlour over a cup of tea and slice of seed cake, instead of talking through rusty bars in a place that stank of rank bodies.

They didn't stay long. Alf had said almost nothing to his dad, just looked at him with horror, and soon the gaoler was rattling his keys and clearly wanting them to go. Alf had reached out to grasp his dad's arm then, and Uncle Fred had reached through the bars to shake both boys by the hand in turn. *As if we are men,* thought Bill.

'Happy Christmas,' they'd all said, but none of them believed it would be.

Then they left Uncle Fred in that awful place. Bill and Alf said nothing to each other as they followed the gaoler back down the corridor, nothing until they were back outside that big gaol door.

'We've got to get him out,' said Alf. 'Did you see . . . ?'

'Yes,' said Bill.

In the courtyard of the gaol there had been a platform with a gibbet on it, its looped rope swaying slightly.

'How do we do this dragon show, then?' said Alf. 'It's got to pay for a lawyer. It's *got* to!'

'I know,' said Bill. 'It will.' He thought of that stone grin wrapped in sacking and hidden in the chicken run. Was it laughing at them, or was it a helpful smile?

Chapter Twenty-Two

The next day, Bill and Alf were in the chicken run, looking at Croccy and working out how to do their show, when a shout from out the front let them know that Dad was home.

'You'd best go for now,' Bill told Alf. 'But I'll be round yours as soon as I can.' And then Bill hurried inside to see Dad with his arms around Ma. Bill stood awkwardly in the doorway, then Dad noticed him.

'Billy, my boy! I got the early train and walked from the station. Couldn't keep from my family a moment longer than I had to!' He rummaged in his bag. 'I've brought presents.' There were his wages, which he handed to Ma, but he also gave her a paper bag.

'What's this?' she said.

'Candied cherries, Sal. Sweet and good, and made by

Cook from the big house.'

Ma sniffed. 'And how old is 'Cook'? Is she handsome?'

Dad laughed. 'She's fat and old, with only one good eye. Not a patch on you, Sally, girl! And I paid her for those cherries, so don't you worry.'

For Bill there was a good penknife that folded into its own handle. Bill held it in his hands, and didn't know what to say. He'd never had such a fine bought present. It was perfect.

'Whether you work indoors or on the land, any man needs a knife in his pocket for cutting string or sharpening pencils or paring fruit and the like, as well, of course, as cutting pens,' said Dad. 'I've put your initials on it, see. WE for William Ellwood, same as me.'

'Thank you,' said Bill, closing his fist around it, and slipping it into his pocket. Then Dad produced something else with a shy sort of grin. He'd made a wooden rattle with a rounded hollow head with a bead inside it that clonked when you shook it. It was beautifully smooth.

'For the baby,' said Dad. He gave a little nod to Bill. Ma must have told Dad that Bill knew about the baby. What else had she told him in her letters? 'I carved this from a piece of lime tree that was shed in that storm a while back. It's given me something to do of an evening when I was missing you the most.' He gave Ma an apologetic look. 'I know it's too early really, but I've been thinking of you and the babe so much, Sal.'

Ma smiled, wrapped the rattle in her best hankie, and stowed it in a drawer. 'How are those chickens?' said Dad, hobbling towards the back door. 'Let's take a look at them, Billy. Your ma tells me that they've both stopped laying.' So Dad and Bill went out the back, as Ma made tea.

'What's that lump of stone doing in there?' said Dad, pointing at the fossil head in the chicken run. So Bill told him. He told him all about the fire and Croccy and Uncle Fred. Dad listened to it all, and then he crouched down and stroked the stone grin as if it was a live animal.

'Well, I'm blowed!' he said. 'I'm sure we can make a fine display of that, if it's to help poor Fred in his predicament.' He glanced over his shoulder. 'Perhaps it might be best to keep it all quiet from Ma just for now. I don't want her getting worked up and worried over anything more. Come on, let's have that cup of tea and then we can get started on your show.'

It was good to have Dad back.

'So, what can we add to the head to make a proper show of it?' said Dad, once he'd persuaded Ma to sit with her feet up for a bit.

'We really need a whole body,' said Bill, thinking of the fossils in the museum. 'That would look better than just a head.'

So Dad and Bill went to fetch Alf. Then Alf went off to the butcher's while Dad and Bill took a bucket of clay from the diggings spoil heap. They brought it back home, and used tools from the shed to shape vertebrae. Alf arrived a short while later with an armful of real bones.

'I swept the butcher's floor clean of all the old bloody sawdust in return for these big ones,' he said.

'William?' came Ma's shout from indoors.

Dad put a finger to his lips. 'Do it all quietly, lads,' he said. 'I'd better go inside now.'

Bill, hands numb with cold as he shaped the wet clay, nodded towards the tin bath hanging on the shed wall.

'You can make some mud in that to soak those bones in, and then they'll perhaps come out looking properly old to fit with the head.'

'That's clever!' said Alf.

By the time the feeble winter sun was sinking, they'd assembled and left to dry most of what they needed to make their dragon.

'Christmas Day tomorrow,' said Bill. 'I won't be able to get away until after lunch.'

'Nor me,' said Alf. Then he looked at the ground. 'They don't let you visit the gaol on Christmas Day. Poor Dad.'

'We'll get him out soon,' said Bill.

* * *

Christmas Day meant a service in church, with most people from the village there. The Widnalls and Lilleys and Nutters, Mrs Buckle and her children, and others from the big houses sat in the front pews, all in best bonnets and shawls, top hats on laps or under pews. Miss Snelling, on her own, was in a middle pew. The Ellwoods sat towards the back, with the Dilleys and other trade or labouring families. Auntie Lil and the Smith children were in the very back pew, overflowing across the aisle to fill both sides. Bill looked over his shoulder and grinned at them. Ma, wrapped in her best paisley pattern shawl, looked forwards and didn't turn. Dad did turn and give a little nod of the head by way of a Christmas greeting.

Lil Smith looked old, thought Bill. The Smith children were unusually still and quiet. *How much of the village would be praying for Uncle Fred today?* wondered Bill. He certainly would be. And praying for his baby brother or sister too.

Ma's belly bulged noticeably with the baby now. She sat with one hand resting on the bump. *Just as she used to rest a hand on my head when I couldn't get to sleep,* thought Bill. She hadn't done that for a long time. Ma was sat up very straight on the hard pew, but she was as pale as milk. Bill couldn't tell whether or not she was listening to what the vicar was saying. Reverend Buckle was talking about baby Jesus being born in the poorest of places. That might comfort Ma, thought Bill. Her baby could be born in better than a stable, at least. Dad, cap in his hands on his lap, was listening earnestly to all that Mr Buckle said.

There was a chicken for lunch; Betty. Dad had wrung her neck, plucked and drawn her last night. He'd done the same to Flop, the very last chicken, a bit bigger than Betty, and he'd told Bill to take Flop round to the Smiths as a gift for their Christmas dinner.

'No need for you to tell Ma,' he'd said, a finger to his lips. 'I'll tell her about it when the time is right.' But Ma had stepped outside to put the potato peelings in the compost heap, and she'd caught Bill holding the prepared, dead chicken.

'Billy! What have you got there?' she'd said, and he'd braced himself to be labelled sneaky and a thief and a disappointment. But she didn't do that. 'It's your dad giving it to Lil, isn't it? Come in quick, before the heat's all lost from the house,' she said. Then she handed Bill a little package. 'Give that to your aunt too, will you? Just pass it over when they open the door. No need to go in. Then knock on Mrs Coddle's door and tell her she's expected here for Christmas dinner at midday. Nobody should be on their own for Christmas.'

And Bill had gone, the dull glow of love for his mother suddenly flaring warmer and brighter than it had for some time. So it was disappointing that she couldn't bring herself to greet her sister in church.

It was Bill, under instruction from Ma, who did most of the final preparation of their Christmas lunch. Ma's feet had swollen with the walk to and from church, so she sat with them propped up on a stool. Dad laid the table, and Bill chopped vegetables and opened a pot of relish. Ma had stuffed the chicken earlier with onion and breadcrumbs, and now it was roasting, filling the house with a smell that made Bill's stomach rumble. At midday Mrs Coddle arrived, bringing a bottle with her.

'Elderberry wine,' she said. 'It'll do you good, Sal. And you too, William. Shall I give Billy a little?'

'No,' said Ma. 'He's only a boy, after all.'

Bill was content to let the adults chatter about Dad's work as he concentrated on the tasty food, savouring the last forkful of chicken and gravy-soaked potato. Then he sat back and looked at his parents and Mrs Coddle, all of them going red-cheeked with the warmth of the fire and the effect of the wine, and he felt content.

There was even a plum pudding to enjoy after the roast chicken. It had been steaming in the pan on the range and filling the house with sweet fruity smells for a couple of hours now.

'Can you serve it up, Billy?' said Ma. 'On my best platter off the dresser. That's it. Warm it with water from the kettle, then unwrap the pudding onto it. Lovely!' said

Ma, and she giggled. Dad looked at Bill, and they both laughed too. *We should give Ma elderberry wine more often,* thought Bill. 'Old Mrs Widnall sent us that pudding, William,' Ma told Dad. 'Just as if nothing had changed.'

'That was kind of her,' said Dad, and Bill supposed that it was, but he felt the familiar twist of guilt that came every time there was a reference to the Widnalls.

The pudding was good. Richly full of raisins and candied peel and almonds and cherries and brown sugar and maybe a spot of brandy. Bill concentrated on its flavours and the nice feeling of having a full belly, as Mrs Coddle talked. She'd had more of the wine than either Ma or Dad had.

'I saw you yesterday, didn't I, Billy, taking something over to them Smiths?' she said. 'I stopped you, didn't I, Billy?' Mrs Coddle turned to Ma. 'I made him show me what he was carrying, and it was one of your old chickens all done ready for cooking, Sal.' Dad looked sheepish, but Ma lifted her chin.

'I know about it,' said Ma. 'Old Mrs Widnall isn't the only one who can forgive and forget.'

'Oh.' Mrs Coddle looked disappointed that she wasn't surprising Ma with news of the chicken, and that pleased Bill. But on Mrs Coddle went. 'Know what that chicken parcel brought to mind? It took me right back to that tiny babe, fresh born, wrapped in a flour bag and sent over the road, just like that chicken, but –'

'Well, that was a grand lunch, that was,' said Dad, scraping his chair back from the table.

Thank goodness for Dad, thought Bill. The last thing he wanted to round off that delicious meal was another of Mrs Coddle's horrible baby stories, especially with Ma having a baby inside her that might or might not become another of her tales. 'That was a treat, Sally, love,' said Dad. He lifted Ma's hand nearest him, and kissed the back of it. 'Billy and I have something to see to while the light holds, but we'll be back to wash the pots. So you two ladies settle by the fire and have a game of cards, eh? Perhaps enjoy some of those candied cherries. You make sure Sal keeps her feet up, will you, Mrs Coddle?'

'But where are you two off to?' said Ma. 'Not one of the pubs?'

Dad laughed and blew her a kiss. He'd never been one for pubs. Except for today. And that was not in the way Ma might have expected.

Chapter Twenty-Three

They *were* off to a pub, in spite of Dad's laughing at the suggestion. Bill and Dad went to the Red Lion, but they didn't go inside it. Dad had spoken to the landlord there and got permission to use the yard beside the pub for the dragon show, and they met Alf outside, as arranged.

'What's the idea?' said Alf.

'Those two big gates will make a kind of entrance,' said Dad. 'We'll make a frame behind that, and then cover it with fabric to make a tent. Billy, I thought we could use those old curtains that Mrs Foulkes gave your ma a while back. She hasn't got around to using the good parts of them yet, and they're large.'

'The big yellow things? All faded and tatty edged?'

'That's it. I reckon they'd make fine tent walls. And we can put something that'll keep the water out better on the top in case of rain. I've got a tarpaulin we can use.'

'Could we put little flags at the corners? They do that at fairs,' suggested Alf.

'Why not?' said Dad.

Alf grinned. 'This is going to be the best show Grantchester has ever seen! When do we put the dragon together?'

The landlord of the Red Lion liked the idea of an attraction that would draw visitors to the pub. He kept popping out to see how the work was going. Men going into the pub for a drink stopped to ask about it too.

'There's going to be a show,' Bill told them. 'Tomorrow. Thruppence to come inside and look. You'll see a real dragon.' Somehow the idea of a dragon seemed more exciting than a crocodile, and who would know the difference anyway? Maybe it really *was* a dragon.

Bill thought of what Mr Seeley had said about the Frenchman thinking that Mary Anning had made up a creature from bits of all sorts of different ones, and that seemed a good idea. He also remembered how changing the look of the dahlias had counted as cheating, and that made him uneasy. But they had to make a good show of it for Uncle Fred's sake.

It wasn't long before they'd collected the materials and strung up the show tent walls and roof. It was dark in the yellow-walled tent, both because the day was darkening outside and because the curtain walls blocked what light there was left. Bill had put some oil and a new wick into the battered lantern they'd saved from the shed fire. It didn't leak, and lit well, so they used that to light the work of assembling the dragon.

The fossil head was the best bit of the dragon. The teeth and eye holes were clear to see when they were lit up. Bill and Alf lifted the fossil head onto a table with a stool on it, all covered by a black cloth. There were all the still slightly damp, lumpy clay vertebrae made by Bill – small at the neck, growing bigger down the back, then dwindling to really small at the end of a tail in a diagonal line. Bill and Dad had used one of Ma's knitting needles to run a hole right through each one when the clay was wet and now they tied lengths of garden twine through each vertebra in turn, and hung them from a roof pole so that the spine of vertebrae hung at just the right height coming off the back of the head. It took concentration, tying knots in the cold and gloomy light, getting each in just the right place, fifty-two times over.

'Nice knife,' said Alf, as he watched Bill work.

'From my dad,' said Bill, then realized that remark was making them both think about Alf's dad. 'Come on, we've got to make this dragon look like a real skeleton – to impress people and make them send their friends along to see. Pass me that fan. This dragon's going to fly!'

Mrs Foulkes had given Ma the broken, spoked half-circle fan some years ago. It was too torn to use in society, but too good to throw away, and that's why she'd given it to Ma. It was made of a painted paper and lived in a drawer, until Bill had taken it. Stealing, he supposed, and sighed. Why was it that every time he tried to make things right it somehow involved him in doing other things wrong? Bill let Alf use the new knife to slice the paper out of the fan so that the remaining spokes spread like the bones of a small wing. Bill put the ox bones, as legs dangling down from the table. He stitched them to the black cloth to hold them in the right place.

'That looks wrong,' said Alf, pointing.

'It isn't,' said Bill. 'Think about how a hare's leg bones work. They have really big bones sticking backwards for their back legs, with small bones under those big ones that stick forwards. This dragon leaps like a hare!'

'As well as flying?' said Alf.

'As well as flying,' agreed Bill. 'More people are going to pay to see something that's really interesting.'

Bill was aware that there was already a buzz of interest beyond those big wooden gates. Word was spreading about a dragon to be on show.

'We need a poster,' he told Alf. 'Like the one that fortune woman had on her caravan.'

Dad had a word with the landlord, and he gave them

an old sign they could write on the back of, and then put on display.

See back into the past! Meet the Grantchester Dragon! painted Bill, with the brush Dad used for pollinating flowers, and green paint from the shed. After that dried, he used an ordinary goose-feather pen and ink to surround the letters and to draw a swirl of dragon. They nailed the poster to the wooden yard gates.

'How many people have got to pay their thruppences before we get as much money as the market man offered for the fossil head?' said Alf.

Bill had worked that out already, and the result worried him. 'Twenty people,' he said. 'We should easily get that many, don't you think? *And* we'll still have the head fossil to sell when Mr Seeley gets back to his college.'

'How much do lawyers cost?' said Alf. 'What if everyone's spent their money on Christmas? With the diggings having closed early and people not being paid what they'd expected, people might not afford a show.' He frowned. 'We really have got to make the dragon more interesting than anything anybody's seen before. I'm going to add something else to it.' And he pushed out through the gates and away.

Dad had gone home some time before to be with Ma, so, for a while, Bill was alone with the dragon.

'Do you mind being disguised as a dragon, Croccy?'

he asked the fossil head. Croccy's smile seemed to suggest that he was enjoying it. 'It must be better than being kept in the dark, underground, for all that eternity of time. I'll find you a good home after this,' promised Bill.

Alf burst back into the tent, making the lantern flame flicker with the draught.

'I've got fire!' said Alf, holding out a scrap of flame-coloured shimmering silk. He held it against the black cloth so it looked like fire coming out of the dragon's mouth. 'It's me dad's best silk hankie, won in a fight way back when we was in Ipswich. He'd like us to use it, don't you think?'

'How can a skeleton blow fire?' said Bill. But he had to admit it did look good hung from the tent roof by invisible threads so that it seemed to flare from the fossil mouth.

'It makes it look more of a show,' said Alf.

The short midwinter day had darkened to blackness as they worked.

'Light the candles now,' said Alf. 'Just for a moment – we won't waste them – so that we can see how it will look.'

The landlord had given them a pile of candle stubs. They set them now into leftover clay vertebrae as holders, and lit them, placing them around the tent.

'Not too near the sides!' said Bill. Then he stepped back with Alf to admire their work. Grins spread over their faces.

'It looks alive!' said Alf.

'The really strange thing is that Croccy really was living once, a long time ago,' said Bill.

And they both stood in wonder as the candlelight flickered on the head and vertebrae and wing and flame, the shifting light and shadows giving Croccy a feel of movement . . . of breath . . . as if it was also watching them.

Chapter Twenty-Four

Bill got to the show tent before Alf did on Boxing Day morning. The landlord had bolted the gates and said his dogs would guard against intruders, but Bill hadn't slept well for worry that Mr O'Brien had somehow got to hear about Croccy and stolen him. Bill was up before first light to check.

Thankfully, the dragon show was undisturbed. Bill stroked a hand down Croccy's muzzle as if he was greeting Dolly rather than a fossil, but this nose was cold and there was no welcoming nod and whicker.

'It's show time, Croccy,' he said.

'You're barmy, you are,' said Alf, bursting through the gates. 'I've got an empty treacle tin to put all the money in.'

Dad came to see that all was ready. 'Well, that all

looks a treat,' he said. 'I must get on with those jobs that Ma's waiting for me to do. Let me know when you need help taking it all down at the end of the day. In the meantime, I hope you get a good lot of customers.' He put a thruppeny bit clunking into the tin. 'Just to start you off,' he said. 'And to pay for my look at your beast.' He went out through the gate, and then popped his head back. 'Would you let me tell Ma about it now? Maybe even bring her to see it? I reckon she'd be proud. She'd certainly be cross to learn that she'd missed out!'

It would be a relief to know that Ma knew. Bill hadn't liked being kept out of the secret of Ma expecting a baby, and he didn't want to hurt Ma back by doing the same thing to her. Besides, Mrs Coddle was bound to talk to Ma about the dragon show.

'You tell her,' said Bill. Dad would know how to do so in a way that made it all right.

As the day brightened, people emerged from their homes, and Bill and Alf took turns to walk around the village, shouting out, 'Come and see the Grantchester dragon! The great big, fire-breathing, hopping, flying dragon! Thruppence a look. Roll up!'

They didn't say that the dragon show was to get money for Fred Smith, but people seemed to guess it, anyway.

'I'm not paying good money for an arsonist who lost me days of good paid work,' said one man.

But the baker from next door to the Smiths turned up. 'In truth, I'm not greatly interested in dragons,' he told the boys. 'But I'd like to help your father, Alfie. He's more than once slipped me a rabbit for my pot.' He tapped the side of his nose. He paid the second thruppence to jangle into the tin. Through the gates, and into the curtain tent he went, and Alf went with him. Bill, outside, could hear Alf telling him a tale of how they found the dragon.

'It was a dark and stormy night. Nobody with any sense was out under that moon. But Billy Ellwood, he had a feeling. It was as if he was being called.'

'Called?' said the baker. 'Who by?'

'By the beast!' said Alf in dramatic voice. 'Buried deep in the dark, dismal depths of the earth, the beast felt the presence of a boy who knew about stone bones like him.'

'That's Billy Ellwood, all right,' said the baker. 'I saw his little display of fossils in that shed before it got torched by . . . well, by somebody.' He coughed, embarrassed, but Alf wasn't put off.

' "Come!" said the beast to Billy. "Let me out of here!" So Billy, he took this very shovel here . . .'

On the story went. Bill noticed that others heading for the pub could hear Alf's tale from the other side of the big doors. They were stopping to listen.

'That's never a real dragon in there, is it?' said one man to Bill.

'It's a real fossil,' said Bill. 'Touch that fossil head when you go in there, and you're touching history – a beast that lived thousands of thousands, maybe even millions, of years ago.'

'Is that a lucky thing to do, then, touching history?' And the man took coins from his pocket, and paid to go in.

Once the baker came out, his face agape with wonder, telling what he'd seen and heard, more people paid their thruppences, or a penny for children. Dad did bring Ma along after a short while. She wouldn't look at Alf, but she let Bill show her what was inside.

'Quite a show, eh, Sal?' said Dad.

'It is, but not something I'd have in the house,' said Ma. 'Is that my fan? And my curtains? Well, I never! What a thing you've made, Billy!' But she was laughing a little, so that was good.

'I think you boys are a marvel,' said the baker when, later, he came back with a tray of fresh baked buns. 'Sell these for a penny a time,' he said, 'and you keep that money. Alf, tell your dad I done that for you.'

The landlord of the Red Lion was pleased too. 'Here, have a hot pie. You're drawing in custom for me very nicely,' he told them at lunchtime. 'You're certainly giving folks plenty to talk about when they come inside. I've never heard the place so noisy.'

The show was at its busiest by mid-afternoon. Alf,

getting even more into his storytelling role, had gone into the pub kitchen and powdered himself in flour to look ghostly as he told tales which grew a little different and a bit more dramatic each time, about how that dragon came to escape the pit where it had lain under Grantchester through the centuries.

Then, as the day was darkening, a surprise visitor came.

'Mr Widnall!' said Bill, coming out of the gates. 'Oh, and . . .'

'Yes, all of us!' laughed Mr Widnall, waving an arm to indicate not only his mother, wife and sister-in-law in their large skirts, shawls and hats, but a couple of gentlemen too. 'We heard of a Grantchester dragon on show, and couldn't resist.' Mr Widnall put a whole big half-crown into the tin, and waved away Bill's attempt to pay him something back. Alf led the party, two by two, into the show tent. 'As if entering the Ark!' said Mr Widnall.

The Widnall group were shown the dragon and told one of Alf's versions as to where the beast came from. 'Most interesting,' declared Mr Widnall when he came out. 'You do like to put on a show, young Ellwood!'

Bill blushed and said nothing.

'But is the beast real, Mr Widnall, sir?' asked somebody who'd been skulking close by. Bill saw with alarm, that it was Mr O'Brien. 'If you don't mind a fellow asking a gentleman that would know such a thing.'

Bill tensed.

'Oh, some of it is undoubtedly real,' said Mr Widnall, replacing the top hat on his head as he turned to follow his party home.

Mr O'Brien turned to Bill, and sneered, gap-toothed now, 'And where might a boy like you have found a piece of real dragon, I wonder?' Without paying, Mr O'Brien pushed through the gates into the tent, and Bill couldn't do anything to stop him.

'Oi!' came Alf's voice from inside, and Bill stuck his head in to see O'Brien poking at the dragon, setting the vertebrae swinging so hard that one of them dropped off.

'Who'd be fooled by . . .' scoffed Mr O'Brien. And then he stopped, looking more closely at the head. He took up the broken lantern and swung it close to the head, peering and poking. 'Why, that's . . .' He raised his voice so that everyone waiting outside could hear him. 'That's stolen property, that's what that is! You Smiths are all the same, stealing and setting fire . . . Oomph!' Alf had punched O'Brien hard in the stomach.

'My dad did not set fire to that shed!' shouted Alf. 'And we didn't steal this fossil!'

'So it *is* a fossil!' said Mr O'Brien, triumphant in spite of clutching his stomach. 'So where's it come from, as if I didn't know?'

'The diggings,' said Bill, coming in to stand beside Alf.

'Just as I thought!' declared O'Brien. 'So it belongs to the mining company, and you've stolen it!'

'Mr Gander didn't mind us taking other fossils. You've taken and sold fossils from the diggings yourself,' said Bill. 'Did what you took belong to the company? Did you steal those?'

'Oh, you think you're clever,' said O'Brien. 'But just you wait. I've a mind to tell on you. And not only to Mr Gander, but to the company boss of it all!' He kicked the table to make the fossil head wobble. Bill grabbed to hold it safe. 'Maybe the company'll grant me a nice reward for reporting a theft like this.' Mr O'Brien reached a big pink hand towards the treacle tin of money that Alf was clutching. Alf pulled the tin back. Mr O'Brien held on, then suddenly let go so that Alf, the tin and the coins all went sprawling onto the tent floor. Mr O'Brien lifted a foot as if to kick Alf, then snorted a laugh, slammed back through the gates, and shouted at the people outside, 'There's no dragon in there, it's all a cheat!'

'It is not!' said Alf, scrambling up to follow him out.

'Oh!' Mr O'Brien smiled, turning with such menace that Alf cringed. 'So you will give all these good folk their money back if I can prove that isn't a dragon there, will you?'

Alf paused as the people around looked at him expectantly.

'Yes,' spat Alf in fury. 'I'll give the money back if you prove its not real!'

Oh, Alf! thought Bill. He felt sick.

'Might I have a look?' said a gentlemanly voice that Bill recognized, and relief flooded through him.

'Mr Seeley!' said Bill. 'I thought you were away.'

The watching people became still, intrigued to see what such a gentleman dismounting from a big, fine horse might have to say.

Mr O'Brien snatched his cap off his head, slightly bowing towards Mr Seeley.

'Oh, it's all a terrible cheat, sir. Don't waste your money on it!'

Mr Seeley didn't look Bill in the face or answer him. He simply put sixpence into Alf's hand, then smiled at Mr O'Brien and the crowd.

'Ladies and gentlemen, I am from the Woodwardian Museum in Cambridge. I heard word from a friend that a dragon had been found in Grantchester, so I have ridden out especially to see it. May I?' And he stepped through the gates into the tent. Bill and Alf followed, and others, including Mr O'Brien, opened the gates wide so that all could see. Mr Seeley picked up the lantern and used it to study the dragon's body, halting to have a closer look at the head. Then he nodded slightly.

'Well!' He turned to face everyone. 'I can confirm

categorically that this is indeed a fascinating find, and an important one.'

'But it's a cheat!' said Mr O'Brien, stepping close to the dragon. 'Look at those leg bones, would you, sir? They're never the real thing.'

'They most certainly are real bones, and leg bones at that,' said Mr Seeley. 'Although I would question that wing. And the amusing flame coming from the beast's mouth. That, I think, is a piece of fabric. And the vertebrae are a fabrication, of course, but done with skill and accuracy.'

'We did make them,' said Alf. 'You're right.'

'But . . . !' Mr O'Brien was red-faced with anger. 'Surely to goodness –'

Mr Seeley held up a hand. 'That's enough,' he said quite fiercely. Mr O'Brien was considerably older than Mr Seeley, but Mr Seeley was a gentleman who spoke with authority. Mr O'Brien shrank back. 'But I do think that we should close the show now,' said Mr Seeley. And suddenly Mr O'Brien's anger was replaced with servility.

'Oh, I could maybe help you, sir,' said Mr O'Brien. 'I'm a strong man, if a rough one. I could carry that stone head for you.'

'Not necessary, thank you,' said Mr Seeley, holding the gate open as if he was a maid showing a caller out of a house. 'Good day to you.' Mr O'Brien went, and Mr

Seeley closed the gates.

Then Mr Seeley, Bill, and Alf stood in silence beside the dragon in the tent for moment before Mr Seeley pushed one gate open a crack and peeked out.

'He's gone.' He smiled. 'Good. Now, Bill, please introduce your friend and tell me what the real story behind this beast is.'

Between them, Bill and Alf told the tale, this time with none of Alf's dramatic additions.

'Do you know what this jaw is really from?' said Mr Seeley.

'It's like the one you showed me that the girl Mary found at the seaside,' said Bill. 'I remembered it, but not the name. I know it's special.'

'Her name was Mary Anning, and you're almost right,' said Mr Seeley. 'What you saw was a plesiosaur, but this,' he said, touching Croccy's toothy grin, 'looks to be an exceptionally fine example of an ichthyosaur's head.'

'Is that posh for dragon?' said Alf.

Mr Seeley smiled. 'Well, funnily enough a geologist who has written a whole book about ichthyosaurs does call them dragons. His book is called *The Book of Great Sea Dragons*. But ichthyosaurs aren't dragons of the sort that would ever have breathed fire. Those, I am fairly sure, are the stuff of myth.'

'But you told Mr O'Brien –'

'That the leg bones were leg bones. They are. But, as you and I know, not leg bones from a dragon, or any other ancient creature. Are they ox bones?' The boys nodded. Mr Seeley laughed. 'You've put together something quite clever, but of course the real interest is only in that head. What I'm longing to know is, was there a body attached to it?'

Bill made a face. 'We don't know,' he said. 'The trench got filled in.'

'D'you want to buy that head off us?' said Alf. 'How much will you pay, sir?'

'Alf!' said Bill. But that was what he wanted to know too.

Mr Seeley pushed the doors open to let more light in, then he touched the fossil head rather fondly.

'I certainly am interested, Alf, but I couldn't afford to buy it for myself,' said Mr Seeley. 'I'll need to speak to Mr Sedgwick about possibly buying it for the museum. Or I know of other collectors in London or Oxford who would be interested. It will take a little time to find you the best deal to be done.'

'How much time?' said Bill. 'We need the money now for –'

'Will it be for as much as five shillings?' interrupted Alf. 'That's what the market man offered, along with a plucked goose.'

'Ha! Did he indeed!' said Mr Seeley, wiping the stone

dust from his hands onto his trousers in a way that would have made Ma scold. 'Well, I can assure you that this head is worth a great deal more than that. And worth more still if we can find the rest of the creature to make a whole skeleton; a real one this time.' Mr Seeley rubbed his hands together. 'Goodness, this is an exciting find. How lucky that I came back to Cambridge in time, and that a friend happened to have visited Grantchester today!'

Dad came along, as he'd promised, to help dismantle the show, and so he was introduced to Mr Seeley. Together they arranged for a cart to take Croccy's head, wrapped in one of the old curtains, to Mr Seeley's college rooms for safe keeping.

Alf and Bill picked up the entrance money from the tent floor and took the treacle tin to the Smiths' house to count it, with all the Smith children and Aunt Lil standing around the table watching the half crown and sixpences, the thruppeny bits and pennies and halfpennies and farthings all add- up.

'Five shillings, thruppence halfpenny,' declared Bill, and Aunt Lil clasped her hands together.

'Do you suppose that's enough for a lawyer?' she said. 'It's two or three days' worth of a good labouring wage, so surely should pay for an hour or two of a lawyer gentleman? I just don't know until I ask one. But, oh, the story of how you got that money is going to cheer Fred for sure, when I see him tomorrow. You're good boys, the two of you.'

It did feel good to have earned hope for Fred Smith and his family, and to have done it with the help of Dad and even Ma. It gave Bill hope too. Maybe helping others would bring good luck back to Bill's family and help the baby be born strong.

Chapter Twenty-Five

Dad had to return to work at Audley End the next day.

'How long for?' asked Bill as Dad pulled on his jacket and cap.

'Only three more weeks,' he said. 'That'll go in no time. I'll be home well before the baby is born.'

But not before Uncle Fred's trial, thought Bill.

'What will we do for money once this job of yours is finished?' asked Ma.

'Don't you worry about that, Sal,' said Dad. 'We're up to date on the rent now. Something else will turn up, you'll see.'

'The diggings start up again tomorrow,' said Bill, but he knew his wages weren't enough for a family of three, never mind a family of four.

Bill walked with Dad down the road to set him on his

way to the railway station.

'Now, Billy, you get the doctor straight away if Ma gets bad, do you hear? Don't worry about the money for it. Ma's worth more to me than rubies. We'll sell everything we have, if it comes to it.'

Am I worth precious stones to Dad, too? wondered Bill as he watched him go.

It was quiet, and somehow the house felt colder with just Ma and Bill in it. Bill was glad to get back to work the next day.

'How much do you think about things, Doll?' asked Bill, blowing on his hands to warm them enough to do up the buckles of Dolly's harness. Auntie Lil was going to ask about a lawyer in Cambridge today. Mrs Buckle had told Lil that the lawyers would be back after their Christmas break now, and Uncle Fred's trial was set for the end of the week. 'Oh, Dolly, I hope our show got enough money! Or that Mr Seeley can buy Croccy nice and quick.' Dolly's huge head steamed in the cold air. *Yet money shouldn't be able to buy freedom from guilt, should it?* thought Bill. A thing was either right or wrong, without money on one side of the argument making it so.

'Do you wonder why you should do what I tell you to do, Doll, even though you're bigger and stronger than I am?' said Bill, leading her towards the washpit. Dolly, plodding the line he guided her, seemed perfectly content with doing as she was told. *Perhaps she's wise,* thought Bill. *Perhaps I should be like Dolly, content to do what the grown-ups and gentry tell me to, day after day after day until I get old and die.*

'I want to see more of the world,' he told Dolly. 'Is that wrong?' He thought of Uncle Fred, locked in gaol, trapped in one place. Bill watched a crow flying overhead. The bird was free. It might get shot or trapped, or eaten by a fox, because freedom could be dangerous. But Bill still ached with suddenly wanting to experience more freedom like that. What would he do with that freedom? He'd find things out. He'd go and see the sea and the cliffs showing layers of land. He'd understand the world more if he saw more. But for now he went round and round and round with patient Dolly.

'Oi, Bill!' shouted Mr Gander. 'Hand Dolly to George, there. I want you over by the gate, sharpish.' Bill was surprised to see Mr Seeley already at the gate, along with some other gentlemen and Mr Gander. Mr O'Brien, passing by with a barrow full of soil, gave Bill a sneering look that made Bill feel uneasy. Perhaps those gentlemen were here to arrest him for stealing the ichthyosaur from the coprolite mining company. 'Bill,' said Mr Gander, hat off, and a hand gesturing towards an elderly gentleman with white hair. 'This gentleman here is the Reverend Professor Adam Sedgwick. He and his students have come about some fossil that you apparently found.'

'The ichthyosaur, Bill,' said Mr Seeley, nodding encouragingly. 'I've shown the fossil head to Mr Sedgwick.'

'Indeed,' said Professor Sedgwick, smiling kindly at Bill. 'It's a very fine specimen, and we would very much like to search for the rest of the creature in the hopes of making it complete, if that is agreeable to the mining company. Can you show us exactly where you found it?'

Bill let out the breath he'd been holding, and smiled back. He wanted to see Croccy's body too. This was exciting!

Bill showed the gentlemen exactly where in the filled-in trench he'd found the fossil head, and which direction it was pointing. As they talked, Bill could feel Mr Gander tense with questions about the mess made of that trench, and he could also see Mr O'Brien watching and listening. It felt to Bill as if Mr O'Brien was a cat waiting to pounce, and he was a mouse.

Mr Seeley took Bill to one side while the other men were examining the trench. 'There's much to be discussed about ownership of this creature, Bill, but I'll see to it that you get fair payment, for the discovery if nothing else. It was you who were bright enough to spot the ichthyosaur and realize its importance, and that must be recognized financially.'

'Thank you,' said Bill. 'But it was my friend Alf too. Him and me together.'

'Understood,' said Mr Seeley.

But how much would that payment be? wondered Bill. He felt it would be rude to ask a gentleman that question, so he didn't.

Bill called at the Smiths on his way home from work, wanting to hear news of how Auntie Lil had got on with the lawyer. Alf snatched open the door and came outside, his fists bunched and his eyes red, and he set off, walking fast to nowhere in particular. Bill, hopped a step to catch up, then walked quickly alongside him.

'It's all no good!' said Alf. 'Mam went to the lawyer gent that Mrs Buckle said to go to and to tell that she'd sent her, but that man, Mr Noble, he liked her money enough to say 'yes' to working for Dad but he says he can't do no good for him!'

'Why not?' said Bill.

'He says there's too much against Dad. All the things everyone's been saying. You know, how Mr Lilley saw him before anyone else at the fire, and Dad had a lantern so they say he must have used that to make the fire, all on account of losing his job and being angry at the company. You can see how it looks!'

'How it looks is wrong!' said Bill.

''Course it is,' said Alf, breathing hard to keep back tears.

Poor Uncle Fred.

'There's just one thing that Mam's clinging to now,' said Alf. 'And that's that Mr Noble said he was almost sure he could get Dad time in gaol instead of hanging. But it might still be transportation for him.'

'To where?' said Bill, thinking how empty his own house was without his dad.

'Australia, Ma thinks. We'd likely never see him again!'

Bill's thoughts seethed as he made his way home to Ma. He felt fury at what was happening to Uncle Fred. Excitement that more of the ichthyosaur might be found. And that nagging ache of worry about Ma and the baby. He opened the door to find her in her chair, blankets and shawls all over her but the fire out. She was shivering so much her teeth chattered.

'Ma, you're freezing!' said Bill, grabbing the coal bucket to fetch fuel to make up the fire again. 'You've got to keep warm!' He made the fire and he warmed some soup. And then he told Ma about what Alf had said about Uncle Fred.

'Oh, Lil,' said Ma. 'Poor, poor Lil.' Ma wouldn't eat the dinner Bill prepared. 'I've got no appetite,' she said.

'You must try,' said Bill. 'It'll warm you, if nothing else.'

Ma took a sip of soup, then put her spoon down. She hugged her shawl around herself and rocked in her chair, a whimper coming from her every now and then. Bill didn't know what else he could do to help her, but he couldn't just sit and listen to that sound of despair. So he went out the back to sort the mess of things from the dragon show. All the fake dragon parts and candle nubs had been wrapped in one of those yellow curtains, and dumped out there at the end of Boxing Day. Now, three days later, the curtains were spoiling, and Bill knew that Ma still wanted to use the good bits from them when she was fit. At least he could undo that bit of damage to her.

In dim moonlight, Bill lifted a side of the yellow curtain, tipping out the crumbling clay vertebrae, the bones, and sooty old lantern from the burned shed, and he wondered if any of those things were worth keeping. He crouched down and picked up the lantern. He could feel the big dent at one corner that made it unstable when placed on a surface. Could that dent be knocked out? Somebody must have thrown it very clumsily to dent it quite so much. Bill froze still a moment, his mind whirling with new thoughts as he looked at that lantern. It was a fancy sort of a lantern, and not what you might expect in a workmen's shed. Somebody must have thrown it into the shed to give it that dent. Throwing a lantern like that would start a fire! And this certainly wasn't Fred's lantern!

Shaking, Bill stood up, holding the lantern up to see it in silhouette against the inky night sky. It had an ivy leaf pattern cut into its sides. Yes! He knew exactly who had started that shed fire! But would anybody believe him? They must!

Bill ran.

Chapter Twenty-Six

'Alf! Auntie Lil!' Bill shouted, pushing through into the crowded, fuggy, dark room full of Smith children and washing and . . . 'Oh!'

A lady dressed in a large maroon skirt that filled a good share of the room stood in front of small Auntie Lil. The size of the skirt meant that the Smith children were pressed against the walls, up the stairs, and onto each other's laps. All were strangely quiet, intent on that big-skirted woman. It was Mrs Buckle.

'Oh, Bill,' said Auntie Lil, smoothing down her own tired old skirt. 'Mrs Buckle has brought us a nice fruit cake. Isn't that kind? She came to ask about how things were with the lawyer and Fred. Isn't that good of her?'

No! is what Bill wanted to shout out, but he didn't. He stepped forward to stand face to face with Mrs Buckle, and he took a deep breath, then held up the lantern.

'This is yours, isn't it, Mrs Buckle?' he said. Bill thrust the rusty battered lantern right at Mrs Buckle, who made a strange strangled sort of a noise and backed away, tripping over Smith children. Baby Mops started to wail.

'Bill!' said Auntie Lil. 'Take that filthy thing outside!'

'But it belongs to Mrs Buckle, doesn't it, Mrs Buckle?' said Bill, staring unblinking at her. Mrs Buckle wouldn't look him in the face. 'Mrs Buckle left it somewhere by mistake . . .'

'I don't know what's got into you, Billy Ellwood,' said Auntie Lil, stepping over and reaching for him. 'But out you go – now!' With surprising strength, Auntie Lil grabbed Bill by the back of his jacket, and shoved him out of the door. Alf pushed past his mother to follow Bill out.

'That's the lantern from the dragon show, isn't it?' said Alf. 'The one that was left after the fire in the shed?' Now he grabbed Bill just as his mother had. 'Was it her?' he asked. 'Mrs Buckle? How could it be? Did she set the shed on fire? Why? How d'you know? Nobody'd ever believe it, would they?'

Before Bill could answer any of those questions, Mrs Buckle came out of the Smiths' door, hurrying up the road back to the vicarage. She was clutching her shawl tight to her chest, bonneted head facing down.

Bill stepped out in front of her. 'Mrs Buckle.'

'Go away, you nasty dirty –'

'This lantern.' Bill thrust it at her again. 'It *is* yours, isn't it?'

'No, no! It certainly is not,' said Mrs Buckle, but she still wouldn't look at it. She was pushing the lantern away, hurrying on up the road. But now Bill and Alf were trotting on either side of her.

'The lantern was in the burned shed,' said Bill. 'It was the burning oil from this lantern that set the shed on fire, wasn't it? Thrown in there by you!'

'Oh, I remember!' said Alf. 'It's your lantern from by your big posh Vicarage front door!' He was shouting at her now. 'And you'd let my dad be hanged dead and forever when it was *you* that made that fire!'

'I didn't! I wouldn't!' sobbed Mrs Buckle. She stopped, and hid her face in her hands. 'I made sure that your mother got a good lawyer. I . . .' She shook her head, realizing what she had said. 'Leave me alone! Those fossils are the work of the devil!'

The boys stopped still, stunned by her confession. She walked briskly away, but they had their answers.

'Well, that proves it,' said Alf.

'Yes,' said Bill. 'We can go and tell them in the courtroom at your dad's trial tomorrow. Everyone will recognize the lantern as being from the vicarage. And we're not the only ones who saw it in the barn after the fire.'

'But will they let us say that in court?' said Alf. 'Will they listen to us instead of Mrs Buckle, who is grown-up and a lady? She's friends with that lawyer, remember. Oh, I bet she can get out of it even now!'

'The truth must be stronger than lies, mustn't it?' said Bill.

'Give me that lantern,' said Alf. 'I'm not letting go of it until Dad's free.'

Chapter Twenty-Seven

Bill was startled awake early the next morning by somebody thumping on the front door below. It was still dark, but he got out of the warmth of bed, stepped down the ladder to the room where Ma was sleeping, then down the stairs to the main room. He opened the door to two surprises.

'Alf!' said Bill. Then, 'Snow!' Everywhere had a strange glow of whiteness in the dark, and snow was still falling. Then Bill noticed the silly sort of look on Alf's face. 'What?' Had Alf gone mad? Bill pulled Alf inside and closed the door.

'It's Dad!' said Alf, waving his hands and almost shouting.

Bill's stomach lurched. What had happened to Fred now? Had those desperate men in his cell hurt him? The court couldn't have hanged him already, without even a trial, surely?

But Bill saw that Alf was smiling.

'Dad's home!'

'Home?' said Bill. 'He hasn't run away from gaol, has he? How could you ever escape that place?'

'No, you daft thing, they let him out!' laughed Alf. 'It worked! Do you see? What you found out about snooty-bloomers Mrs Buckle. She must've told somebody something last night after we saw her, because they've dropped the case against Dad.'

'What, in the middle of the night?'

'Yep!' Alf nodded. 'They just told him the case was dropped, and shoved him out into the night. Told him to forget all about it and get on with life . . . meaning don't ask any questions, Dad reckons. Anyway, he walked home from gaol with no coat and no light through the night as snow came down. He fell in a ditch. He's a right mess! Wet, and needing a shave. Mam's feeding him with every bit that's left of that cake that the Buckle woman brought last night. She's wrapped him in all of our blankets to get him warm. And, well, he's free, Billy! I had to tell you.'

Bill felt something of the tightness inside him relax. He picked up the poker and knelt at the fireplace, coaxing the banked-up coals into life to warm them.

'Does that mean that it'll be Mrs Buckle who will get

the gibbet or be transported, then?' he asked. He wasn't sure how he felt about that. Would they have to appear at her trial and show the lantern that would condemn her?

'Don't be a donkey! She's a lady, isn't she, so nothing bad'll happen to her. I told you, we're to say nothing now that they've let him go. Dad doesn't even know why he was let off, but I bet it was because of Mrs Buckle. Do you think she told the vicar what she'd done? Confessed? And maybe he had a word with Mr Lilley, paid him off or something so that he'd drop the case?' Alf held his hands out to the warmth from the fire. 'Why do you think she set that shed on fire, anyway?'

Bill shrugged. 'She must have done it because she thinks that fossils make what the Bible says wrong. I suppose she can't bear to think anybody'd not believe what her husband says in church. "Work of the devil" she said to us, didn't she?' He smiled. 'And guess what didn't burn to nothing in that fire she made? The fossils!'

'Ha! But the lantern didn't burn either,' said Alf. 'So what was that the work of? I'm keeping that lantern forever. It's my lucky lantern. Unless you want it, Billy? It's more yours, really.'

Bill shook his head. 'No, you have it.'

So they wouldn't have to go to court now, he thought, as he waved Alf off down the road. He could join Mr Seeley and his men as they dug for Croccy's body, unless the snow meant that wouldn't happen now. Bill yawned. He felt properly happy; happy that Uncle Fred was back home and safe, happy that more of his ichthyosaur would come out from its deep, dark burial through the ages. Maybe now that they didn't need more money for Uncle Fred there would be money from the fossil to make everything all right once Dad was home? If he could just keep Ma and the baby safe, maybe everything could come good again.

Bill took a cup of hot tea and a slice of bread and jam up to Ma before leaving for the snowy diggings field.

'Uncle Fred's out of prison,' he told her as she heaved herself to sit up. 'They aren't going to try him in court after all. He's free.'

'Oh, Billy!' said Ma, clutching her throat. 'Does that mean they'll be coming for you instead?

Bill almost threw the cup of tea at her. 'No!' he shouted. 'Of course not! How could you think that?' Then he saw how small and frail she looked, that baby bump so big, and he knew that he mustn't be angry with her, even though he was. He also knew that it would shake Ma even more if he told her who had really set fire to the shed. She probably wouldn't even believe him. So Bill took a breath. 'We're digging the fossil's body today. The ichthyosaur. You keep warm, Ma. Perhaps just stay in bed today. There's snow outside and it's cold. I'll come home at lunchtime to stoke up the fire and heat the broth Mrs Coddle brought round yesterday.'

The excavation of the ichthyosaur took several days. The gentlemen persisted in digging in spite of the snow and cold. Old Mr Sedgwick rode out to see how things were progressing, but it was Mr Seeley and a couple of gentlemen undergraduates, looking strangely different in rough clothes and boots, who did the digging, along with two of the men they'd hired from the company. They dug the trench wider where the ichthyosaur's body was, removing all the earth from on top of where the body must be, so there was less danger of collapse than there had been. The cold weather helped keep the earth stable, and Bill noticed that Mr Gander instructed that wooden props be used to hold up the trench walls in a way they never bothered with for the coprolite digging. Bill should have been with Dolly at the washpit, but he was so distracted with interest in what was going on in the trench that Mr Gander gave up on telling him to go back to Dolly.

'Would your friend Alf Smith look after Dolly, just while the fossil dig is going on?' he suggested. Alf was pleased to, especially since school hadn't started up again yet so he was free to work. To everyone's surprise, Uncle Fred was back at work too. It seemed that the Reverend

Buckle had told Mr Gander that he would personally assure that Fred Smith would not cause any further trouble.

'I don't think even Mam would promise that about him!' said Alf. 'But those Buckles are scared enough to say anything to keep Dad sweet just now. Guilty consciences, that's what.'

Ma had heard from Mrs Coddle that 'poor Mrs Buckle' was ill, and had left the village to stay with a sister for a while. Bill said nothing when Ma told him that. He didn't trust himself not to burst out with the whole truth of it all, so he kept his mouth shut.

Bill was useful to the university men, not just in showing where he'd found the fossil, but in doing odd jobs too. They sent him to the pubs to fetch hot drinks in bottles wrapped in cloths to keep the heat in. They asked him to fetch tools or to put small fossil finds somewhere safe. Every so often Mr Seeley invited Bill down into the reinforced trench to see that the rest of the ichthyosaur was being laid bare for the first time in what he said was probably millions of years. Bit by bit, nearly all of the bony structure of Croccy's body was revealed; it was much longer than Bill, and shaped rather like pictures of dolphins he'd seen. Bill felt as if the creature was being slowly born from a very different time into the world that Bill knew. If only Croccy could speak and talk about the world he had lived in here when it was so different!

'See that?' said Mr Seeley, a few days in to the excavating. 'That's one of the ichthyosaur's paddles.' There was a mass of small bones, together making a paddle shape. 'Like a Roman mosaic, do you see? It's the creature's hand, of course.'

'It doesn't look like a hand,' said Bill.

'There are no fingers, it's true,' said Mr Seeley. 'But the bone structure is just the same as if there were fingers, but supporting a paddle shape rather than a hand like yours or mine.' Bill spread out his hand and looked at it. Mr Seeley sat back on his haunches and brushed soil from his trousers. 'A bird's wing, a bear's paw, a human's hand, or an ichthyosaur's paddle; they all have the same bone structure. Some would say that shows that one designer, God, made them all. Men such as a chap called Huxley say that those bone similarities show that all creatures developed from the same origin. They evolved differently according to their circumstances.'

'So do I have the same thousands-of-times-great-grandparents as this ichthyosaur?' said Bill.

'I don't know about that,' said Mr Seeley. 'All these dinosaur and sea creatures laid eggs, of course, while mammals such as you and I are born from our mothers. With that in mind, you might say that fish and dinosaurs have more in common with birds than with us.'

'But why have animals changed so much since the ichthyosaur lived here?'

'They probably evolved tiny bit by tiny bit as the climate changed, or the food supply changed, and goodness knows what else changed. Creatures adapt to the environment they find themselves in because those best suited survive and breed, while those less suited die out.'

'But living things can change faster than that,' said Bill. 'My dad showed me how beetles come out of eggs in the earth, and they come out as worms before they turn into beetles, all in a few days. Caterpillars turn into butterflies, so that's another one where something that can't fly turns into something that can. That's in just one lifetime!'

'True.' Mr Seeley was stamping his booted feet to warm them and kick off the mud. 'But even more extraordinary than those examples, Bill, are human embryos. Can you pass me that pasty? And have one yourself.' The pasties were fresh from the baker, and very good.

'Thank you,' said Bill. 'What is an embryo?'

'It's the name we give to a baby while it's still developing inside its mother. I've seen some, pickled and preserved, and looking remarkably like fish.'

'How?' said Bill.

'Well, the human baby – you and I in our time – starts life with a tail, and with brachial tubes like gills, and no arms or legs. As the embryo baby's head forms within the womb, its eye holes, which have been on either side of the head, as a fish has them, move to the front of the head, making a human face. If those halves of the head don't exactly meet, you get a cleft palate or a hare lip.'

Bill went quiet, thinking of the baby inside Ma. Might it have something wrong with it, like Dad's club foot?

All afternoon, Bill thought about the world's millions of years of life. He felt as though his sight was clearing, letting him see back and back in time. And yet he could hardly look forward at all. He knew that he would get bread pudding for dinner today, because he was going to make it, but what could he know beyond that? The seasons would come and go, round and round, for certain. But what about him? Bill felt tiny in the hugeness of time and space, almost as if he was floating. *Two parents made me,* he thought. *Four grandparents, eight great-grandparents, sixteen great-great-grandparents, and on and on forever behind me.* It was odd to think that one day he might make new people, maybe, far into the future, hundreds of them might be descended from him, and most of them he'd never even know about. The baby inside Ma was the only person in the world who was the same mix of all those ancestors who had made Bill. *Will he, or she, be like me?* he wondered.

Light was fading when one of the undergraduate gentlemen came upon a surprise.

'Come and see this, Seeley!' he called from down in the trench. 'I think we've got another ichthyosaur!'

Mr Seeley and Bill ran to the trench to look. Mr Seeley carefully brushed away soil to reveal more.

'Well, that certainly *is* a surprise!' he declared. 'There's a smaller ichthyosaur as well as your big one, Bill. Much smaller. Head just the length of my index finger.'

'But there are some of my big ichthyosaur's bones on top of it and behind it,' said Bill, looking at the shapes in front of him. 'The little one is *inside* Croccy!'

'Fascinating!' said Mr Seeley. 'Well, we'd best leave it, now that the light's going. We'll excavate it properly tomorrow. Cover it with that sacking for now, Bill. Bill?'

But Bill wasn't listening. The small ichthyosaur was *inside* his big one. It was being *eaten* by Croccy! Cannibalism! Did that explain Croccy's big grin? Bill felt disgusted. Like Mrs Buckle, his ichthyosaur had been pretending to be something nicer than he was. Well, now Croccy had been found out!

'I'm going home,' said Bill.

'Billy!' It was Uncle Fred, calling to him as he stomped across the field. 'Are you unwell, lad? You look at bit –'

Bill turned away, but Uncle Fred followed him. 'I wanted to say thanks, Billy. Alfie said it was you that . . . you know.'

'That's all right,' said Bill, and he hurried on, thinking

how things weren't really all right at all. *I'm like Mrs Buckle and the ichthyosaur, too,* he thought. *Uncle Fred thinks I'm good, but it was my fault that Mrs Buckle set fire to the shed. It was my fossils that upset her. So it was my fault that Uncle Fred almost got hanged. As well as my fault Dad lost his job.* Bill wanted to run from himself as well as from the excavation.

It was cold in the house, and dark. The fire had almost gone out. *Ma must be upstairs,* thought Bill, as he added fresh coal and puffed bellows to get the fire going again. Then he heard a strange animal kind of a noise that made his mouth go dry with fear.

'Ma?' Bill dashed up the stairs. 'What . . . Oh, my lord!'

In the slight light of dusk through the window, Bill saw Ma on her hands and knees on the floor. For a moment he thought that she must be looking for something she'd dropped. Then pain clenched her body tight as a fist, and her grey face turned to Bill, her mouth open and moving, but silent. There was terror in her eyes.

'The baby,' whispered Bill.

Chapter Twenty-Eight

Bill saw the wet puddle on the floor under Ma. He saw that there was blood too. He'd watched puppies being born at Wright's Farm once. He knew how it worked, but he still didn't quite believe that a whole baby could come out of Ma the same way. Ma didn't look as if she believed it either.

'It's only a baby being born, Ma. You've done it before.' Bill stroked Ma's back as if she was Dolly.

Ma groaned a deep agonized sound from somewhere deep inside herself. 'Get Mrs Coddle,' she panted. 'Go, Billy, please!'

So Bill was running again, this time down the stairs, out of the house, along the road, and into the lane where Mrs Coddle's slumped old cottage was. *Oh, please help me, Mrs Coddle!* he thought. *Please know what needs to be done for Ma. I don't know about babies and birth!*

'Mrs Coddle!' he shouted. 'Mrs Coddle! Ma's having the baby!' Bill thumped on her door. 'Mrs Coddle!' At last she opened it. Her hair was awry, her eyes wandering. *Oh no!* thought Bill. 'Ma needs you,' said Bill. 'Put on your boots. Quick!' Mrs Coddle looked slowly at Billy. She had a silly sort of smile on her face. Then she laughed. Bill spotted the bottle on the table behind her. 'Are you on the gin, Mrs Coddle?'

'Only a little drippy-drop to ease the pain in my wrists,' she said, pushing her hair up. It tumbled straight down again. 'No harm in a drop of good . . .'

'Put your feet in these.' Bill picked up the boots that were by the door. He held one open for her to step into, as if she was a small child. 'You've got to come. There's blood on the floor under Ma, and she's hurting that much!'

'Deary-dear,' said Mrs Coddle, pulling a face. 'That ain't good. No. Why, I remember a woman not long back who bled before the baby came, and she died along with the baby.'

'Oh, please hurry!' said Bill, struggling to tie her string laces. 'If Ma dies . . .' Bill couldn't finish that thought, and he certainly didn't want to hear about dead babies or dead mothers just now. Mrs Coddle giggled and ruffled Bill's hair as he finished tying the last boot.

'Look at you, all of a doo-da! Don't you worry, Billy boy, first babies never hurry. Why, I remember one poor soul, only a girl really, who took five whole days and nights, heaving and sweating and swearing something awful before her baby came out. That one died too.'

Bill concentrated on grabbing a shawl and wrapping it around Mrs Coddle's shoulders as he pushed her out of her house and shut the door.

'Tiny scrap, that baby, the size and look of a rat,' went on Mrs Coddle. 'That girl had another babe the next year. Big fat one this time. It came out easy, between her putting porridge to cook and it being cooked and ready to eat. Called that baby Goldilocks on account of the porridge.'

The hobble-run along the snowy road seemed to sober Mrs Coddle up a bit. She held on to Bill to keep herself from slipping on the snow that had turned icy with night-time cold, and he pulled her along to hurry her.

'Right,' said Mrs Coddle, as they stepped through the doorway and stamped snow off their feet. 'Up there, is she? Set the kettle to heat, and find some clean cloths. Sheets or summat.' Mrs Coddle heaved herself up the stairs, and Bill turned to set the kettle over the fire. But then Mrs Coddle called out, 'Give us a hand up here, Bill, quick!'

Bill went up, but held back when he saw Ma still on all fours, and groaning.

'She can't stay on the floor, panting like a blessed dog,' said Mrs Coddle. 'We've got to get her onto the bed. You lift that side, Bill . . .' Ma arched in pain as Bill and Mrs Coddle lifted her thin arms to heave her up onto the bed. Then she fainted, pale as the sheets she was on.

'Best thing,' said Mrs Coddle. 'Gives her a rest.'

Bill pulled Ma's skirts down over her legs, making her decent.

'That won't help with this job, will it?' laughed Mrs Coddle. She rummaged up Ma's skirts. 'Not long now. Not long at all.' Then she slapped Ma's face. 'Wake up now, Sal. You've got a baby to push out.'

Bill stood, looking in horror at the floor.

'All that blood,' said Mrs Coddle, looking too. 'That ain't good, not at all.'

'Shall I fetch Auntie Lil?' said Bill. 'Or the doctor?' That's what Dad had said to do.

Mrs Coddle puffed out. 'No time, boy,' she said. 'Get a good sharp knife, quick as you like.'

'A knife?'

'To cut the cord when the babe comes out!' she said.

Bill reached into his pocket and pulled out the penknife that Dad had given him.

'That'll do. Now bring up hot water in a basin,' said Mrs Coddle. 'Ooh, now, here we go.'

Ma was waking to the pain that was clenching her.

She was grunting. Bill knew that Ma would hate him to have seen her like that. He went downstairs and poured scalding hot water from the kettle into Ma's best china basin. Trying not to slop it, he carried the basin of water upstairs, and backed into the room, placing it by Mrs Coddle's feet.

'Right, Bill.' Mrs Coddle's voice was sounding scared now, and that terrified Bill. 'Now get me some snow in a cloth.'

'Snow?'

'Snow. Go on, boy! Quick as you like!'

Was Mrs Coddle properly mad? If only Dad was here! With Mrs Coddle part drunk, and all those tales of babies and mothers dying, Bill wasn't sure what to think.

He found it a relief to step outside into the night-time, snowy coldness that made his teeth chatter. He'd grabbed a clean cloth from the drying horse as he went out, and now he scooped snow into it. The snow was soft and easy to push together into a block, cold enough to numb Bill's fingers. One of the Smith children was running along the road with a basket.

'Vicky!' shouted Bill. 'Tell your mam that my ma's having the baby. Tell her we need her quick.' Then he shut the snow and darkness outside, and hurried back up the stairs towards the sounds that frightened him, and the metallic smell of blood.

'It's out,' said Mrs Coddle, pointing to a glistening blue thing that lay still on the sheet. 'It's a goner, blue and dead as I've seen them before, and now your Ma's bleeding bad. Give me that, and we just might save her.' Mrs Coddle placed the wrapped snow on Ma's tummy, low down. Bill's eyes slid from the startling sight of his Ma's naked tummy, puffed and pale, to the sheet over her legs, scarlet with fresh blood. Then he realized what the slimy blue thing on top of that sheet was.

'The baby?'

'Take it away,' said Mrs Coddle. 'It'll upset your ma to see it.'

So Bill quickly wrapped the small, still, bluey-purplish baby, slippery with blood, in one of Dad's shirts that was on a shelf near the bed. He wrapped the baby as if it wasn't dead, leaving its face exposed because that felt right, and he hurried downstairs with it.

Where was he supposed to put a dead baby? Bill crouched by the fire, warming himself, and rocking, rocking as he tried to make sense of what had happened, of how he felt. He looked at that baby face, with its perfect nose and mouth, and eyes that were closed and looked asleep. Bill remembered how the farm puppies had come out of the mother dog, Meggie, seeming to be dead, but Meggie had licked and cleaned and nudged them until they took breath and opened eyes and lived.

So Bill blew warm breath onto the baby's face. He used the sleeve of Dad's shirt to wipe the face clean of the white stuff that clogged the baby's nostrils and eyes. Then he rubbed the baby's skin as he rocked it in his arms by the fire, comforting himself, comforting the floppy, dead baby, humming to it to shut out the sounds that were still going on upstairs. And he thought of how badly he had failed – how Dad had told him to look after Ma, and how now the baby was dead and Ma might die too.

And then the baby in his arms moved.

Chapter Twenty-Nine

The baby's face crumpled, its mouth opened, and a small cry, like the bleat of a lamb, came out of it.

'Hello,' whispered Bill, his heart beating fast. 'Hello, you funny thing!' He sat himself down on a chair, and laid the baby on his lap in front of the fire, rocking it with his knees as he spoke into that violet, cross little face, and he rubbed and gently kneaded the baby's tiny arms. Bill had once sat and watched a daisy flower when the sun first touched it in the morning. He had watched as the bud unfurled, throwing out its white petals in a fringe around the yellow middle, and it had happened fast enough for him to see the movement happening. Now he watched as the baby blossomed. Its colour changed from blue to pink. Its mouth worked, and then its limbs came to jerky life. 'Come on,' encouraged Bill.

'You've got to live, cos you've got a daddy who needs you, and a ma who needs . . .' Bill broke down, hot tears pouring down his face as he lifted the baby to his shoulder, and rocked and patted and soothed until the baby let out a sharp, high-pitched cry to properly greet the world.

'Billy?' came Mrs Coddle's voice from upstairs. 'You've never got that baby to live, have you?' So Bill carefully, tenderly, carried the baby back up the stairs.

'You've got a baby, Ma!' he told the grey face on the pillow, and he held the baby to show it to Ma, and Ma to the baby.

'Well, I never!' said Mrs Coddle. 'Well, I say "never", but there was that babe born to Nell Goodwin, few years back, and that one –'

The door downstairs was banging open.

'Sal? Billy? It's me, Lily. Can I come up?'

'Auntie Lil,' said Bill. Would Ma mind her sister coming into her house? To see her in this state? But Ma might be dying, and Lil was kind and knew about babies. 'Up here,' called Bill.

Lil and Mrs Coddle worked together to care for Ma. Bill took the baby up to his attic, and lit a candle. He sat on his bed, staring, staring, marvelling at the tiny, solid weight of the new life in his hands. He saw now that the baby wasn't just 'a baby'; it was a very particular little person. Bill unwrapped the baby a little. There was the purple ropy twist of a thing coming from its belly. And there was something else lower down.

'You're a boy,' whispered Bill. 'A brother.'

Bill wrapped the baby snug again, and he rocked and rocked him until Auntie Lil came to him with a cup of warm milk. Billy handed the baby to Lil, then, and he sipped the milk as she rocked the baby in her arms. She had tears pouring down her face as she looked from the baby to Bill.

'Is Ma . . . ?' began Bill.

'She's resting now,' said Lil. 'Best thing for her. Mrs Coddle's with her, and Fred's gone off at a run for the doctor.' She smiled at Bill. 'For all that your Ma holds herself so high, she's just flesh and blood the same as all of us, when it comes to it, poor soul.' She kissed the baby on the forehead. 'But she's got you to live for now, hasn't she, poppet?' *And me,* thought Bill. *And Dad.*

Ma had a fever by the time the doctor came. For the next two days, Auntie Lil and Mrs Coddle seemed to be living in Bill's house, caring for Ma. Mrs Coddle wanted to sit with the baby, telling Bill stories about other births and other babies, but Bill wanted the baby to himself. It seemed that the baby wanted that too, always settling better for Bill than for Mrs Coddle. They warmed cow's milk, mixing in a little honey, and fed that to the baby, and he'd always take more when it was Bill holding him with one arm, and holding a horn spoon of the warm milk to his mouth with the other.

'He needs a name,' said Mrs Coddle. 'Can't talk to him proper until he's got a name.'

'My dad'll give him a name,' said Bill. He longed for Dad to come. He'd written a letter to him the day after the baby was born, scratching the words out with an old goose feather quill and the bottle of drying-up ink, but sending it with a proper penny stamp.

Dear Dad,
The baby is born. It's come early and is small.
Ma is ill. Please come home.
Your son, William.

Bill didn't ever normally use his proper name, William, but somehow it felt right in a letter telling big news. He'd made sure that the address at Audley End was clear on the envelope. How long would it take to get there, and then for Dad to get home?

'You probably don't realize it, Billy, but it's Monday today,' said Mrs Coddle. 'You should be back at your job, you know. If you don't turn up, they'll go and give it to somebody else, and that's not what your Ma needs now.' Mrs Coddle was clattering Ma's pans in the sink as if the house was her own, putting them back onto the wrong shelves. But Bill didn't dare leave the house, leave the baby, leave Ma. Ma sat up in bed some of the time now. She'd even tried feeding the baby, but Mrs Coddle said the milk with honey was doing more good to the baby than Ma was.

Ma's face was flushed with fever still. She hardly said a thing, didn't even seem to notice when Bill was in the room with her. Auntie Lil was back and forth from her own home, washing and feeding and caring for her sister, leaving her own children to be looked after by Fred and the big ones. Alf came and poked at the baby, making it cry. He tried telling Bill about how Mr Seeley and the others had lifted the ichthyosaur fossil bodies, the big one and the little one inside it, out of the ground now, but Bill wasn't interested. All he could think about was the baby and Ma and Dad, and that didn't interest Alf. The only person in Grantchester Bill wanted to be with just now was the baby. And he wanted Dad.

During those days there was an awful dread in Bill that he didn't understand but couldn't get away from. The doctor said that Ma was getting stronger, but that things could still take a sudden change for the worse in such cases. That was part of Bill's dread. The doctor's bill was a dread too. But there was something more. Life just felt as fragile as a rose that's been picked and left in water for a few days, and that was now ready to drop its petals at the slightest movement; perhaps maybe drop them even if nothing else moved at all. Bill felt as if his life, and the lives of those he loved, would all fall apart forever if he stopped concentrating on Ma and the baby for a moment. He rocked the baby against his shoulder, loving its warmth, not minding its smells and mess, marvelling at the way it already responded to talk, following Bill's face, yawning when Bill yawned.

On the third day, Bill went down the road to get bread from the baker's, as Auntie Lil asked him to.

He only stopped concentrating on home for a few minutes, but it was long enough for the petals of his life to fall.

Chapter Thirty

Bill came into the house through the back door, closing it quietly in case Ma or the baby were sleeping. Mrs Coddle and Auntie Lil were talking in the main room.

'Has Sal given that poor mite a name yet?' asked Mrs Coddle.

'Yes,' said Lil. 'He's to be William, after his father.'

'But that's my name,' said Bill, coming into the room. 'You can't have brothers called the same name!'

Auntie Lil froze, staring at Bill. Mrs Coddle put her knobbly hands over her mouth and giggled, then pointed at Bill. 'But you and the babe aren't brothers, are you, Billy Ellwood?'

'Mrs Coddle!' warned Lil. 'You've no business –'

'What do you mean?' Bill glared at Mrs Coddle, and she giggled back at him. *She's been at the gin again,* thought Bill. *Is she making up some story?* No, he realized slowly, because Lil had gone pale and was trying to distract him by thanking him for the bread and asking if he'd like a fresh slice. But Bill wasn't to be distracted from this, because it was clearly important. 'Mrs Coddle, what do you mean, I'm not the baby's brother? Is Dad not his dad?' Bill felt sick. Everything was shifting and falling, just as he'd dreaded.

''Course he is!' said Mrs Coddle with a whoop of delight. 'Do you really think your ma's gone off with a man who wasn't her husband?'

'Mrs Coddle!' Lil was trying to steer Mrs Coddle towards the door now, awkwardly because of the baby on her shoulder, but Bill dodged in front of them, barring the way.

'Tell me!' shouted Bill. 'The truth!'

'Shh!' said Aunt Lil. 'Don't wake your Ma.' Bill opened his mouth to demand the truth again, but Lil held up a hand. 'No, Billy, love, we can't tell you. That truth isn't ours to tell.'

'I'll ask Ma, then,' said Bill.

But Lil put out a hand to stop him from going upstairs. 'No,' said Lil. 'No, don't. Not in her state now.' She looked deep into Bill's eyes with her face that was so like Ma's, and yet different. Lil took a deep breath. 'Billy, love, you were an adopted baby.'

And Bill knew it was true. That was why he wasn't the son that Ma wanted him to be. That's why he didn't properly fit in his own family!

'You never guessed that, did you?' giggled Mrs Coddle, unable to help herself in spite of having a hand over her mouth as she said it. She pointed at Auntie Lil. 'You're really hers. Her's and Fred's. One of twins.'

And Bill knew that was true too. Fred and Lil felt a part of him somehow.

'I'm that baby wrapped in a flour bag that was carried over the road,' he said.

'That's it,' laughed Mrs Coddle. 'Little scrap, snatched away the moment you was born. "Don't show it to me," Lil said. "I can't bear to see it." I had to wrap you in a flour bag, because baby gowns and blankets couldn't be spared when there was another baby about to be born. That next baby to come out was Alf, of course, and they kept him. Soon as Alf and what comes after were out, I took the flour bag of baby, hidden under me shawl, to Sal, who was waiting. Fred never knew there was two babies. Only Lil and Sally and William ever did. And me, of course.'

Lil was leaning against the wall now, holding the baby, and crying as she looked at Bill. Bill looked from her distraught face to Mrs Coddle's gleeful one.

'Well, maybe I'd better be on my way, eh?' said Mrs

Coddle. Bill stepped aside, and Mrs Coddle opened the door. 'Ooh, look, there's your dad coming up the road, Bill!'

But Dad wasn't Bill's dad. Ma wasn't truly his ma. Bill looked at Lil. She turned her head away. Lil, his true ma, had chosen Alf, and sent Bill away without even looking at him, wrapped in a bag like something from the grocer's. And she couldn't even look at him now. Even though she was clutching Ma's baby as if it was her own . . . the baby with the warm body and sweet-smelling hair that wasn't his brother, after all.

Bill bolted out of the back door.

Chapter Thirty-One

Bill ran through the meadows, avoiding the road that Dad was walking up.

The snow was gone now, but the world was full of freezing fog that clung around Bill's head in a way that made it ache. Bill ran to the one place where he could find uncomplicated companionship . . . to Dolly.

Dolly was standing at the field gate. Bill climbed the gate, put his arms around her neck, and sunk his face into her solid, warm, woolly neck. Dolly reached her big head around to nuzzle Bill's side. Bill stroked down Dolly's hard head to her velvety, warm muzzle. Her big whiskered lips played with his fingers as her warm breath plumed into the cold, foggy air. *Dragon breath*, thought Bill, but he knew it was really steam made from drops of water so tiny they could hang in the air. *How can air turn to water?* wondered Bill. *Dad might know.* But Dad wasn't his dad. Dad had a new, real, son to tell things to now.

'They're all liars,' Bill told Dolly, stroking and stroking her nose. 'They don't want me. I don't want them, either. Let's go away from them all, Doll.'

Dolly nodded her big head up and down, with a snort that seemed to Bill to be agreement. It was easy to step from the top of the gate onto Dolly's great broad back, one hand clutching a handful of mane, the other reaching down to unloop the rope that held the gate in place. Bill made clicking sounds with the side of his mouth. 'Come on.'

Bill had only sat on a horse a few times before. Dolly's back was so broad his legs spread so that he was almost lying on her. She lumbered into the gate, pushing it open, and then they headed away from the field. One of the Manor Farm dogs appeared, yapping, out of the fog, startling Dolly into a trot. Bill clung on to her mane.

'Whoa, Doll!' There was another dog now, both dogs yapping at Dolly's heels, and the trot turned to a canter like a giant, slow, rocking horse, and that was easier to ride. It got them away from the dogs too, and soon they were cantering through fog that looked the same bright greyness in every direction. Bill's eyelashes had droplets on them, making him blink. The damp air was cold, but the speed of cantering was exhilarating. It felt to Bill as if he was anywhere or nowhere. Time had stopped for him. Place had disappeared. He was free in a limbo, cantering from his troubles.

Dad would be home now, meeting his real son.

Bill thought how much he had loved that baby, how he had loved Ma anew for creating that new life, and squeezing his brother out into the world . . . as Bill must have been born from inside Auntie Lil.

An image of another small being inside a larger one came into Bill's mind, and he suddenly realized something that made him shout out into the fog.

'Croccy's a ma! She's a woman, not a man! She's having a baby, not eating one!' Bill laughed. Now, suddenly, he did have somewhere to go. Mr Seeley had said that ichthyosaurs laid eggs like lizards and fish did. He was wrong! Bill must tell Mr Seeley what he'd discovered.

Bill rode Dolly over the meadows, following the river downstream towards Cambridge where the gas lights made the fog glow, leading Bill on towards Sidney Sussex College. He tied Dolly to railings nearby, then went into the porters' lodge and asked,

'I want to call on Mr Seeley, please. Mr Harry Seeley, the museum man.'

'I don't think Mr Seeley would want –' began the porter, wrinkling his nose at the sight of Bill, sodden by the damp fog and now shivering in the cold.

'Ah, but yes he would, thank you, Mr Jenks,' said Mr Seeley, appearing around the corner. 'I've come to fetch my package, if you please. Bill, what can I do for you?'

'I've found something out, Mr Seeley. About my ichthyosaur and that little one. I reckon –'

'Come to my rooms,' he replied as Mr Jenks handed over a brown paper package. 'There's a fire in the grate, and I dare say tea could be brewed and crumpets toasted. Then you can tell me all.'

Mr Seeley led Bill into a stone courtyard where the fog was beginning to sparkle as sun broke through to pick out its drops. The carved stonework rising up around Bill made him feel as if he'd stepped into a fairytale kind of a place. He followed Mr Seeley up broad wooden stairs to his rooms.

Then Bill told Mr Seeley how the little ichthyosaur could be the big one's baby. Wasn't that more likely than it eating one of its own kind? Wasn't Croccy a mother rather than a cannibal?

'She must be having a baby, do you see?' said Bill. Mr Seeley did see.

'Bless me, I do believe you're right!' Mr Seeley lifted his hands upwards, then brought them to either cheek with a little laugh. 'Gracious!'

'Have you ever seen a baby born?' said Bill.

'Well, no, I haven't,' said Mr Seeley. He pointed a finger

at Bill. 'The real excitement here, Bill, is that your fossil discovery is showing us that ichthyosaurs weren't like all the other ancient large creatures that we've studied. Your ichthyosaur hasn't laid an egg, as dinosaurs appear to do. She was giving birth like a mammal, like a human being, indeed. That is quite astonishing.'

'So her giving birth is like those hand bones, showing that humans really are related to ichthyosaurs?'

'That might be so,' said Mr Seeley. 'Gracious, how exciting! Well observed, William Ellwood! Will you take sugar with your tea?'

Bill didn't reply.

'What is it?' asked Mr Seeley.

'I'm not William Ellwood,' said Bill. 'Not any more. There's another one now.'

'You're going to have to explain that to me,' said Mr Seeley, settling back in his chair to munch a hot crumpet dripping with melted butter.

So Bill told it all, and by the end, when he told of Dad coming home, but Dad not really being his dad, he was crying.

'Plenty of people have been brought up by fathers who weren't their biological parent, you know,' said Mr Seeley. 'The job of a parent is more in the caring for a child than the bringing it into the world, I'd think.'

'Jesus's dad Joseph wasn't his biological dad, I suppose,'

said Bill. And that set Mr Seeley laughing. Somehow Bill's crying turned to laughing too, so neither of them noticed the door open, and Mr Jenks the porter usher in two visitors.

'Billy?'

It was Dad.

Bill froze, staring at Dad.

Alf was beside Dad, grinning. 'I told him you'd be here,' said Alf. 'I knew it.'

'Bill?' said Dad again. He sounded scared. 'Won't you come home, Bill?' He held out his arms, and Bill walked into them, to be enclosed by Dad's hug. Biological dad or not, Dad was Bill's dad. That hadn't changed after all.

'See?' laughed Alf. 'I knew it would be all right.'

Chapter Thirty-Two

'Oh, Billy!' said Ma when he came in. She was downstairs, sitting in a chair. She was holding the baby, but she got up and thrust the baby into Dad's arms as she reached for Bill, and he knew then that she was his ma just as much as Dad was his dad, and, oh, that was a surprise and a relief. 'I'll explain everything, Billy,' she said. 'Everything.'

Ma told Bill what had been secret for so long. She held his hands and his gaze and she told how she and Dad had longed for a child. How there had been pregnancies, but, time after time, they always went wrong, and there never was a baby born who was strong enough to live. She told how she and Dad had worked to make a nice home with nice things in it, but how they longed for a child to share it with. And through all those years, Lil and Fred, living in Grantchester too then, were having baby after baby. More children than they could afford to feed and clothe well. So when Mrs Coddle felt Lil's tummy and said she was almost sure there were twins on the way this time, it was Lil who offered one of those babies to her sister. Sal had been pregnant again, but had lost that child too. 'Don't let on to anyone that you've lost the baby,' Lil had suggested. 'You can take one of mine, and nobody will ever know any different, not even Fred.'

So that's what was arranged, and that was what happened. But Ma was so scared that the truth would come out that she and Dad had paid Lil and Fred money to let them move away to Suffolk. 'I made them promise not to come back,' said Ma. She glanced at Lil. 'But then they did, and I was so frightened . . .'

'But I didn't let on, did I, Bill?' said Auntie Lil. 'The children never knew you was more than a cousin. No more did Fred.'

'So, they're all my brothers and sisters?' said Bill. 'And Alf's . . .'

'Your twin,' said Lil. 'The two of you were born either side of midnight, so you've different birthdays.'

Bill looked at Alf.

'Don't look at me like that, Billy boy!' said Alf. 'It don't make no difference to me, one brother more, even if it's a brother from a wipe-your-boots kind of a house!'

Then he swung an arm around Bill's neck, and wrestled him to the floor.

'Who do I live with now?' asked Bill a bit hesitantly, as he got up again. He was surprised that Ma grabbed and gripped tight hold of his arm.

'With us, of course, Bill. This is your home. You're my Billy who I love – I love! Don't you leave me! Please, Billy!'

'But you've got the baby now,' said Bill. 'You've made him a William Ellwood, and he's the real one.'

Dad cleared his throat, and addressed Bill as he rocked the baby in his arms. 'Billy? William Frederick Ellwood? I heard that we wouldn't have our baby at all if it hadn't been for you, saving his life. Baby William is yours just as much as he is ours, because you gave him life too. And, of course, you're his family brother.' Dad passed the bundle of baby into Bill's arms. The baby was awake, frowning as it tried to focus hazy blue eyes on Bill's face. 'That William name is a silly thing,' went on Dad. 'It was just that your ma had it fixed in her head that a blood son should be named after me. We don't have to call him that.'

'It's for your dahlia nursery when you start it,' said Ma. "William Ellwood and Son", remember?'

'But that doesn't –' began Dad.

'He can be William,' said Bill. 'I don't mind, just so

long as he doesn't turn into a Bill.'

'Then you give him a name too, Billy,' said Ma. 'A name to go between William and Ellwood.'

'That's a good idea!' said Dad. 'Go on, Bill, anything you like!'

'Ichthyosaur,' said Bill.

'I beg your pardon?' said Dad.

So the baby was called William Ichthyosaur Ellwood.

'It does sound distinguished. A proper gentleman's name,' said Ma. 'And we don't need to use that full name in everyday sort of life.'

Mrs Buckle walked out of the christening when she heard the name, but the vicar didn't object.

'He's William, really. Just William,' Ma told people. But soon everyone but Ma was calling the baby Ichthy, and then just Itchy.

Bill went on being Bill or Billy. He was only William if he was in big trouble. He was Ellwood, but he was also loved and teased and fed and included round at the Smiths' crowded house. He was everybody's. If he wanted to get away from the noise and muddle of both family homes, he went and talked to big, strong, gentle Dolly. People in the village might point and say things behind their hands about him, after Mrs Coddle's gossiping got spread around to tell the story of the baby given away from one sister to another, but Bill didn't care much. He wasn't going to be in this village forever.

Mr Seeley said that Bill had the makings of a scientist. Mr Seeley said that being a scientist would mean going to new places and meeting new people and having new ideas by watching, noticing things, asking questions, and then finding answers. Bill belonged to two families now, but he also felt more free.

'Not like you, fat Itchy,' he told his baby brother. 'You've got to stay put and be the "and Son".' Because Dad really was planning to start his own dahlia nursery, now that Mr Seeley was saying that they would get "a handsome sum" for the discovery of the two ichthyosaurs.

As spring greened the world outside, Bill found himself back in the cramped little school room, squashed on a bench between Ted Dilley who smelled bad, and Jim Pauley who sniffed. Alf was there too, and some more of his Smith brothers and a couple of sisters. Miss Snelling, and her lessons, were the same as ever. But now Bill didn't twist around to gaze out of the window so much. He had his head down. He was busy forming his letters in lines of copperplate writing. He was learning his spellings and sums. He would stay in the village for now, seeing Itchy grow and helping Dad with his dahlias for the nursery. But Bill knew that the more he learned in and outside school, the further outside the village he would eventually go, and that was exciting. He'd already gone to a museum in London with Dad and Mr Seeley, to see a display of his ichthyosaurs that had his name – *William (Bill) Frederick Ellwood* – on the label as the person who had discovered them.

Bill thought of that often.

It made him grin just like Croccy.

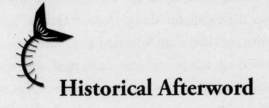

Historical Afterword

Grantchester is a real village just outside Cambridge. For centuries, the life of people in that village revolved around farming. As well as farm workers, there were blacksmiths, bakers, butchers, washerwomen, wives and others who supported those who farmed. But in the 1850s, something extraordinary happened. Coprolites were discovered, and suddenly village fields could earn their owners far more by being dug for coprolites than they be could in growing plants or animals for food. So mining companies came and dug for coprolites. Some people got rich, new people arrived, the landscape changed, and ideas changed too.

The word 'coprolite' was made up by the Reverend William Buckland when he discovered lumpy 'nodules' inside the fossil skeleton of an ichthyosaur in Dorset. Those nodules were stomach contents, and some of them looked like, and were, poo. So Buckland named the nodules after the Greek for 'dung' (*kopros*) and for 'stone' (*lithos*). Some coprolites *are* fossilized poo, but most are simply mashed-up bones and scales and teeth and shells that have come together over millions of years to become hard lumps that accumulated in a 'coprolite bed' layer in the earth.

Why did people mine for coprolites? Because coprolites contained phosphate, and that made it a good fertiliser (or, as they called it then, 'manure') for growing larger and better harvests of crops. They ground down the nodules and treated them up with sulphuric acid (which they called 'vitriol'). That made a powder that would dissolve in the water in soil, and so could be absorbed into plants through their roots. Bigger food crops were needed to feed the growing population of people working in factories and building railways as the Industrial Revolution changed much of Britain.

In 1859, five acres of Grantchester land were rented from King's College in Cambridge who owned it, and coprolite mining began in the village. In April 1860, seven more acres were added. That included land that Mr Samuel Widnall and his mother had been renting for growing flowers.

By 1860, fossils of interesting ancient creatures had already been found by farmers and brick makers in the area. Bones of brown bear, wolf and wild boar had been found in clay, and mammoth, rhinoceros, hippopotamus and ichthyosaur fossils had been found in a gravel pit. Those creatures lived in the same area, but at very different times.

By that same time, a number of dinosaurs and other fossils had been found around the world, and people were studying them, working out the sequence of life on earth. In 1859, Charles Darwin's book, *On The Origin of Species*, was published. Darwin's studies of living things suggested that animals and insects and birds and plants had evolved, changing slowly over long periods of time. Other scientists and churchmen insisted that God made the world for mankind, and that mankind must have been there from the moment the world was created. There were great debates and quarrels going on about it all at the time when my story is set. Churchmen got particularly cross when it was suggested that people had evolved from monkeys!

Reverend Adam Sedgwick was the Woodwardian Professor of Geology at Cambridge in 1860. He had been Charles Darwin's teacher, but he didn't agree with Darwin about evolution, even though they both studied fossils. Adam Sedgwick bought ichthyosaur fossils from Mary Anning for fifty pounds, and you can see a cast of the ichthyosaur, and the illustrated letters that they wrote about the fossil, in the Sedgwick Museum in Cambridge, which was named after Adam Sedgwick. The actual fossil is now in the Natural History Museum in London.

Adam Sedgwick's young assistant in 1860 was Harry Govier Seeley who went on to become a great scientist and teacher, notably researching the link between dinosaurs and birds. In the 1860s, he spent a lot of time visiting coprolite pits and washing tanks, and the coprolite labourers knew to save interesting stones for him. You can see fossils he found that way in the Sedgwick Museum.

Mary Anning and her brother began collecting fossils when they were children, in the early 1800s. Living in the seaside town of Lyme Regis, they searched the cliffs and beaches, collecting fossils revealed after storms and tides. At first, Mary collected fossils to sell to tourists, but as she grew up she became a great expert, teaching academic gentlemen things they hadn't known about fossils. She found the first ichthyosaur to ever be identified.

Ichthyosaurs were on earth before dinosaurs were. Unlike ichthyosaurs, dinosaurs did lay eggs. Amazingly, it now seems that dinosaurs evolved into birds. Humans evolved from mammals that evolved from reptiles that evolved from amphibians that evolved from fish! It seems that ichthyosaurs and plesiosaurs (those 'great sea dragons') became a dead end that didn't evolve into anything that is alive today. But people are still working out exactly how evolution has worked and continues to work, so we don't yet have all the answers. It is only recently that scientists have decided that the *pleisiosaurus giganteus* that Mr Seeley said swam like a swan on the water almost certainly actually swam completely under the water. There is much still to be discovered.

Miss Charlotte Snelling was the real village school teacher in the 1860s, teaching up to a hundred children all in one small school room, with just some big girl monitors to help her keep order. Photographs show Miss Snelling with her hair in tight ringlets. Coprolite mining brought more children to the village, and it also brought money that helped to pay to build a much bigger schoolroom which opened in 1867 . . . and that was the school that I went to as a child a hundred years later.

Mr Samuel Page Widnall had inherited a nursery business from his father who was a famous breeder of dahlia flowers. In 1860, Samuel Widnall was living in the village with his mother and his wife at The Old Vicarage. He loved inventing things and making things . . . and he went on to write a story about a dinosaur in the, then, modern world, and I like to imagine that he could have been inspired by Bill and Alf's dragon show!

Village records show that Mr Frederick Lilley farmed Manor Farm. It is recorded that he offered a five pound reward (a month's wages) for information as to who had vandalized the coprolite workers' shed on the farm, but I don't know if that 'vandalizing' included burning it down.

Mr James Nutter was the miller in the village in 1860, and his family were millers there for generations. There was an old Mrs Foulkes in Wright's Farm, and there was a row of cottages called Bugs Row in 1860 Grantchester.

Bill's family is entirely made-up. So are the vicar and his wife. The real vicar at that time, Mr Martin, had a house built for Miss Snelling to live in, and he was one of the people who got the new bigger, better school built for the village's children.

Acknowledgements

I'd like to thank Nicola Skipper from the Sedgwick Museum, who helped me to choose an ichthyosaur as the fossil Bill finds, and who kindly checked and corrected some scientific points in the final story. I also want to thank Melissa Hyder who did a wonderful job of editing this story, and my agent Anne Clark and husband Michael Goodhart, who patiently encouraged it to evolve into the story it now is.

Legend has that if the ravens leave the Tower of London, then monarch and kingdom will fall.

London, 1666. The Great Plague rages and the city is a dangerous place. Young Nick Truelove blames King Charles II for the hardships he faces and vows revenge. Inspired by the wily cunning of a raven, he bluffs his way into the centre of the King's power - the Tower of London. But as a remarkable friendship grows between boy and raven, a new danger engulfs London. Nick's view of his world and his King is about to change forever.

"Please do not be cross. The fact is, I am to go with
Fa to Canada. It is my idea, and not his. Mama
always said that one should live every moment of life.
That is what I am doing."

Ida's mother has died, leaving her in the charge of her
beloved Fa - only it seems like Ida's the one who does
most of the caring. When Fa decides to travel to the
Klondike in search of gold, leaving Ida in the care of
her Grandmama, Ida knows she must find a way to go
with him. The sights and sounds of the journey and
the hardships they face will push them to very limit of
human endurance - and change them forever.